Opeꓸꓸꓸ   sh,
I slid in ꓸꓸꓸ   the
room. Altꓸꓸꓸ   her
movement from behind a big ꓸꓸꓸ   her
desk. Maybe she hadn't taken roll yet. I received only a few
evil glares as my fellow classmates caught me sneaking in
late, but they didn't dog me. They didn't want extra
homework, either.

"You're late, Sophie!" Frankie Salas, who sat directly
across from me, announced this to the entire class.

I felt every muscle in my body tense.

Frankie turned to me with a grin.

I couldn't speak, couldn't move, couldn't unstiffen my
frozen face if I tried. All I could do was stare at my tormentor
and think, "Why?"

"Wh...what was that? Someone came in late?" The
teacher's balding head popped up from behind a pile of books
in the corner of the room. It took a moment to register it
wasn't Mrs. Warren talking.

Substitute teacher, Mr. Dallin, or as we so fondly called
him, Mr. Pick-N-Flick, had been teaching since the beginning
of time and he hadn't earned his booger picking reputation
for no reason. He was my oldest sister's math teacher. She
told me he left crusties on her papers at least once a week.
He was our sub for three weeks in my seventh grade
geography class. On two occasions, I'd caught him digging for
buried treasure. He was one reason I carried antibacterial
hand lotion in my backpack.

Another one of Dallin's shortcomings, he had blessedly
horrible hearing and eyesight.

My lucky day.

"No, no, Mr. Dallin. I said you look great, Sophie."
Frankie winked. "Doesn't she look great, Mr. Dallin?"

I felt the heat rise from my chest into my cheeks.

Sophie's Secret

by

Tara West

Sophie's Secret

COPYRIGHT © 2007 by Tara West

Cover Art by *Tamra Westberry*

The Wild Rose Press
PO Box 708
Adams Basin, NY 14410-0706
Visit us at www.thewildrosepress.com

Publishing History
First Climbing Rose Edition, 2007
Print ISBN 1-60154-144-9

Published in the United States of America

Dedication

For my yearbook and newspaper students who encouraged me to write. I hope you are pursuing your own dreams. And for Mary, my number one cheerleader, a young woman now, who is making a difference in the world. I am so proud that I was a part of your lives.

I miss you all.

Finally, for baby Sophia. Your smile is my inspiration.

Chapter One

"Do you remember your first time?" My best friend, AJ Dawson, checked under the door to make sure her mother's feet weren't nearby.

I sighed, leaning against the cushioned, and surprisingly feminine, satin headboard of AJ's twin bed. For the past six years, I'd been trying to erase that awful experience from my mind. "Yeah."

"Who was it with?" Krysta Richards, my other best friend, scooted closer.

I shuddered as an icy chill swept up my spine. "My mom." I focused on one of the millions of Michael Phelps posters on the bedroom wall, trying to shut out that painful memory.

AJ's eyes widened. She pushed herself off of her beanbag chair and sat directly beneath me on her plush white carpet. "What was she thinking?"

I shifted my gaze to AJ's petite, white cosmetic table, which looked ready to crumble under the weight of her athletic gear. "She was depressed about my grandma," I breathed.

Next to the time my chubby butt split my too-tight leotards in ballet class, this was one childhood memory I wanted to forget—my first telepathic experience. Though I heard my mother's voice in my head clearly, she wasn't speaking. She was on the phone, just listening, eyes downcast and shoulders slumped. I thought I was going crazy.

Then the voice was louder, echoing in my skull. *How can I live without her?* But Mom's lips didn't move. After she hung up, she began to weep, and then fell to the floor in a motionless heap. My grandmother had just been diagnosed with terminal cancer and given three months to live.

Although I was just a child, I knew I had been listening to my mom's thoughts.

At about that time, I met AJ and Krysta on the playground. We made unusual friends—AJ was the jock, Krysta was the princess, and until my recent transformation, I was the fat dork.

So how did we wind up as best friends? Our "gifts" drew us together. My friends were my safety net, AJ had visions and Krysta received visits from the dead. Around them, I didn't feel like a freak and we pledged to keep our gifts secret.

Luckily for us, we didn't have these supernatural experiences too often, or we'd have been labeled freaks at school. We just wanted to be teens, trying to survive the pressures of school, parents and fitting in.

Since this was the weekend, we could sit around in AJ's room, listening to Green Day, while forgetting about the outside world. Unless we were interrupted by AJ's mom.

"Whatcha doin'?" Mrs. Dawson, peered through a crack in the door.

"Go away," AJ's two favorite words for her mother.

AJ used this expression on her mom every ten minutes. Like clockwork, we could depend on Mrs. Dawson's unannounced interruption into our privacy. She didn't bother me so much but I didn't have to live with it.

"Such a little snot," Mrs. Dawson sweetly intoned and slammed the door behind her. That was that, until this exact dialogue would repeat itself ten minutes later.

Unless...every so often Mrs. Dawson added a twist to the routine, throwing me smack in the middle. Thank God she didn't do it this time or I would be forced to answer the question, "Sophie, do you talk to your mother like this?"

I would look from mother to daughter, hoping one would give me an out. When neither spoke, they left me with no choice but to answer honestly, "No, Mrs. Dawson."

AJ would roll her crystal blue eyes and say, "Her mother doesn't interrupt us every ten minutes."

AJ's way of saying the word "mother" like it was some venomous, foul stench, always fascinated me. I suppose this wasn't Mrs. Dawson's fault. If AJ and Krysta hadn't been wild children the summer before eighth grade, Mrs. Dawson wouldn't have become such a pest.

That was the summer Krysta's mom ran off with a bail bondsman. Krysta's dad worked nights, leaving no adult supervision at her apartment. Krysta begged us not to tell anyone about her mom. We kept our promise and AJ spent almost every night at Krysta's.

They ran around all night, hanging out with the wrong crowd. I didn't want to be caught up in their trouble, so I stopped answering their calls. They figured it out.

At the end of the summer, they were busted by the cops when AJ asked a guy at the gas station to buy her beer. I thought it was pretty ironic AJ didn't see that coming.

When my mom found out, she put me in private school for a year. I wasn't too surprised by my mom's reaction. She never had much faith in me, not when she could compare me to my two perfect sisters. I guess my mom was afraid I'd be influenced by my friends' bad decisions. What she failed to notice was I had already made the choice *not* to be influenced by them.

After Krysta's dad took up drinking, she found shelter at AJ's house on the weekends. Mrs. Dawson let Krysta stay because she felt sorry for her but she still didn't trust either one of them.

AJ put her head in her hands. "God, why can't she leave me alone?"

Ignoring her question, a question we'd heard a thousand times, Krysta painted her toes and I reached for Krysta's *Cosmo*.

"I wish my mom would buy me *Cosmo*." I couldn't believe I was reading a magazine with sex advice. Like girls did it all the time. I felt a twinge of jealousy that Krysta could read whatever she wanted, and then I remembered all the other crap she had to deal with at home.

"My dad's new girlfriend is only 23. She bought it. Does this pink match my skin type?" Krysta pointed her skinny toes at us; a concerned expression crossed her brow, as if all hope for life's happiness hinged on the color of her nails.

"Pink is everybody's skin type." AJ didn't bother to look at Krysta's nails. She was too busy fuming over her mom's latest interruption. Besides, AJ wasn't the type to be interested in fashion. She'd worn her straight blonde hair in the same ponytail since I could remember. AJ was one of the few girls I knew who could still look good without makeup, which she only wore on special occasions. In fact, if she wasn't such a jock, with her bright blue eyes, perfect little nose, and high cheekbones, she'd probably be the prettiest girl in school. As far as clothes, much to her mother's disappointment, AJ picked comfort over style, preferring to wear old jeans and her softball jerseys.

AJ stretched out on her stomach and grabbed a rubber chicken off the floor. "Do you like his newest girlfriend?"

"I don't know. I guess." Krysta reached toward me and grabbed the magazine, flipping to the table of contents. "Does *Cosmo* say anything about nail color?"

Although her dad couldn't afford many nice clothes, Krysta followed the latest fashion trends by wearing her hair and makeup like Kate Moss or Gisele. She even dyed and straightened her dark curly hair in an attempt to look like the blonde Paris Hilton. Quite a contrast to her large dark eyes and olive complexion. AJ and I didn't have the heart to tell her she looked stupid.

AJ flicked the chicken's head with her forefinger. "I bet it's cool not having your mother around bugging you all the time."

That was a totally insensitive thing to say. I felt it in my bones. I felt it in Krysta's bones, as I watched her hand clench the corner of the magazine, her face expressionless.

We both waited for Krysta's outburst. She said nothing as she set down the magazine and quietly walked out of the room.

"That was a stupid thing to say, AJ." I didn't criticize my best friend often, but this time she needed it.

"Go talk to her." AJ rolled her eyes and buried her face in her pillow.

"No, you go talk to her. You said it." Okay, one of AJ's flaws—she didn't handle feelings well. Raised under the shadow of her jock big brother, she wanted to be like him in every way and that meant having no 'girl' emotions

4

whatsoever.

AJ lifted her head and looked directly at me with widened eyes. "I don't know what to say. You're good at this stuff."

"Try saying 'I'm sorry'. Try asking her if she wants to talk about it."

"No!" AJ twisted her lips in that disgusted scowl, as if I'd just asked her to French kiss Cody Miller. Grody Cody Miller, the kid who was tricked into eating an Ex-Lax bar and crapped his pants on the bus.

Someone had to comfort Krysta. When I realized I had to be that person, anger fueled my movements as I stormed off. I hadn't even taken one step before knocking Krysta's shimmery pink nail polish all over AJ's white carpet. "Crap! Krysta didn't put the lid on this polish."

AJ jumped off her bed and rushed to the spill. "We've got to clean this up before my mother finds out."

"Whatcha doin'?"

Too late.

****

AJ's mom was surprisingly understanding about the nail polish. She only made us promise that in the future, we'd paint our nails in the kitchen.

Krysta came back from the bathroom, looked around, and grabbed some nail polish remover. She cleaned the spill like nothing was wrong. I was a little stunned by her reaction, but relieved I wouldn't have to prevent a confrontation.

The stain came up quickly, but the remover left a horrible smell. AJ and Krysta suggested we move to the living room, but I didn't want to go in there. The Mikes could show up. AJ's brother, Mike #1, and his best friend, Mike #2, were two grades ahead of us and very popular. I couldn't risk telling AJ and Krysta my secret with them around. Even though they went to a different school, gossip knew no limits in my world. I would never be able to show my face again if my secret was revealed.

"Let's just open the window and stay in your bedroom, AJ," I suggested while I climbed onto the bed and slid open AJ's window.

"Why? It smells in here." Krysta fanned her nose, acting like she'd pass out.

"Come on, Krysta, you paint your nails all the time. You're used to the smell. Besides," I hesitated, looking out the window to see if anyone was in the front yard, behind the bushes, or within one hundred yards of hearing distance. "I think I like a guy at school."

Smell forgotten, Krysta and AJ perked up like AJ's Shitzu, Patches, whenever we fried bacon. I feared they'd make too much of a big deal about this. After all, what if they didn't like him, or worse, what if they thought he was out of my league?

"Who's the guy?" Krysta cooed and smiled, recognizing the significance of this momentous event.

Sophie had a crush.

Innocent, awkward Sophie who couldn't even look a member of the opposite sex in the eyes. Crazed dreamer Sophie, who said she'd never ever consider a boyfriend, unless that man was Zac Efron. Self-conscious, self-doubting Sophie, who'd just lost thirty pounds of baby fat last year and was still adjusting to new braces. That Sophie had a crush.

I read the looks in their faces—their widened, amused eyes.

Impossible.

I'd spoken the truth. I didn't know when it began, or how I started liking him, but I was in love with the guy who sat in front of me in English class, Jacob Flushman.

"Jacob Flushman!" They screamed in unison.

Oops. I said that last thought out loud. The cat was out of the bag now; there was no turning back. "Yeah, him." I looked out of the window once more. One could never be too careful about these delicate secrets. If the Mikes found out, they'd tease me for sure. "Please don't tell anyone."

"Jake Toilet Flush?" AJ laughed and landed on a beanbag chair in the corner of her room.

"His name is Jacob. We're freshmen now; AJ, it's time to ditch little middle school names." Actually, we were still in the middle school because the high school was overcrowded. So last year, they turned our middle school into a junior high, keeping us in that juvenile prison against our will.

"Jake has big thighs."

Leave it to Krysta to point out any physical flaws. In her world, everyone should look like they just stepped out of *Cosmo* or *YM*.

I pulled back my shoulders, ready to defend him. "He plays football. Football players are supposed to have big thighs."

"My brother plays football," AJ jabbed, "Jake sits the bench."

"Your brother also has a zit juice collection on his bathroom mirror. People still think *he's* cool." I thought in confessing my crush, my two best friends would have been a little more supportive, but all they did was make fun of him. Their rude remarks cut hard. I liked Jacob and slamming him was like slamming me, too. "I don't see either of you with hot boyfriends, or *any* boyfriends."

"Chill." AJ glared. "You don't have to get so sensitive. I get enough of that from my mother."

"Let's look at his yearbook picture."

I feared Krysta would mention the yearbook. Although I couldn't sense it at the moment, I knew what she was thinking. *Let's look at his huge thighs on the football page, so we can make fun of him.*

Krysta grabbed a yearbook off AJ's bookshelf.

Before she could turn the pages, I snatched it from her.

"Give it back!" She tried to grab it out of my hands.

At only four foot, eleven inches, she was no match for me. Last time I checked, I was five foot six and still growing.

"Only if you promise not to make fun of him." In truth, I hadn't seen Jacob's eighth grade yearbook picture and I was very curious. Jacob had a crew cut, big brown eyes and the cutest little ears. I wondered if he was just as cute last year.

"I promise." She smiled wryly.

Knowing I couldn't trust her, I grabbed her *Cosmo* off the floor.

"Swear on Gisele." I handed her the magazine. Gisele seduced the camera lens with pursed lips.

Krysta placed her hand on the model's face. "I swear."

I handed Krysta the book. She could find his mug

shot quickly. The way she liked to look at pictures, I knew she probably had the yearbook memorized.

Krysta could have done it in her sleep. She flipped open to page twenty-three and pointed directly at Jacob. He had a lopsided grin and the pudgiest cheeks ever.

"Ohmigod!" I screamed, setting off a chain reaction with Krysta and AJ, who'd joined me on the bed.

"Now I see why you like him." AJ laughed and flipped her ponytail. "He lost a bunch of weight like you did."

"He did?" Until now, I hadn't known that. Jacob was new to Greenwood Junior High last year, when I was stuck in Covenant Christian Academy. Knowing this little fact made me like him even more. I was sure he knew what it was like to be teased about weight. He *knew*. Jake and I were made for each other. Now all I had to do was convince him.

But how? Although my friends insisted I wasn't that chubby little dork anymore, I had trouble seeing myself as anything but Sophie "So Fat" Sinora. Although Jacob sat in front of me, he had never turned around to talk or even smile. I doubted he knew my name.

"Hey." Krysta said. "Maybe you can go to Freshmen Formal together."

The dance was only four weeks away. It was supposed to be some kind of a junior high homecoming. Sounded lame, but I still wanted to go. Some of the other girls in school were brave enough to find dates for the dance. I thought about asking Jacob, but I shook at the thought of rejection. "Yeah, maybe." My voice faltered.

I turned and stared at my reflection in the full length mirror hanging on AJ's closet door. I had been exercising all summer, so any remnants of fat had been replaced by toned skin. My hair looked perfect today, but that's because Krysta did it. Any other day, it just wouldn't do what I wanted. I could never get the makeup thing down. My mom said my green eyes and thick lashes were my best asset, although Krysta had them drowning in so much eyeshadow, I could barely see them. This, she said, would make my eyes look like a model's, but I didn't think so.

I tried to smile at my reflection, and then quickly sealed my lips. I hated my braces. Food was always getting stuck in them and they made my lips look fat. Krysta said it was fashionable to have fat lips, but I didn't see anything fashionable in looking like you were punched in the mouth.

I sighed, my shoulders slumping, when I realized I had a lot of work to do. Even though I had lost weight, I still felt awkward in my skin which didn't help my self-esteem one bit.

I had to make Jacob notice me before I asked him to the dance. I knew he wouldn't say 'yes' to a dork. I needed to prove to him and the rest of the school that I was cool. But kids were cruel, and they didn't let old nicknames die easily. So how could a girl get a new reputation?

Chapter Two

Why did the day have to begin with pre-algebra? I should have been in Algebra One, but the counselors didn't have faith in my education at the Christian Academy, so they made me repeat my math class with the bonehead freshmen.

And her. The meanest girl in school—Britney Spears wannabe, Summer Powers.

I hated the clink and clank of her stiletto heels as she sauntered to her seat behind mine. I hated the tons of mascara she wore and the bright red lipstick she also used as rouge for her cheeks. I watched her rub it into her face once while I waited for her to finish admiring herself in her locker mirror. I was waiting because Summer insisted on keeping her locker door wide open, so I couldn't get into my locker, which unfortunately, just like my desk, was right near hers.

She gave her heels one last click for good measure and plopped her butt in the seat behind mine. I waited for it. I knew it was coming. Summer had this annoying habit of resting her feet on the book basket underneath my desk.

No big deal. Most kids liked to be comfortable. I would have done it, too, if Mr. Steinberg hadn't placed me in the front row. That wasn't the problem. Her habit of shaking her feet throughout the entire 48-minute class period was the problem.

I had just completed two weeks of my freshman year, only forty more weeks to go. *Forty weeks of this!* I'd go insane. On the first day of school, it was just a light jitter, like an annoying little fly buzz. I turned around and asked her nicely to stop. She smiled and stopped.

The next day, she started the shaking again. I turned around and reminded her about her annoying habit, but in a nice way, or so I'd thought. She scowled at me and shook my desk harder.

When I was six years old, my biker uncle took me for a ride on his Harley Davidson. My brain jiggled for a week afterwards. This is how sitting in front of Summer Powers felt every morning in pre-algebra. I felt powerless to stop her.

Krysta told me Summer had been in five fights last year; she won every one. I was only in one fight in my life. In sixth grade, Patty Ledbetter called me a brat, so I fought her and I got my butt kicked. If any kid could have been dorkier than me, it was Patty. Her parents worked at K-Mart so getting beat by her was really hard to take. I was the laughing stock of the school.

Trying to concentrate on Mr. Steinberg while my head rattled was difficult, but I didn't need to pay attention. I knew this stuff. I was wasting my time in pre-algebra. Fractions. *Duh.* He had to keep stopping the class because Summer was confused, along with the ten other special eds who kept raising their hands. "What's a denominator again?" Were people really this stupid?

I couldn't stand it any longer. I had to see my counselor. Without wasting another aggravating minute, I raised my hand.

"What is it, Sophie? I thought you understood fractions." Mr. Steinberg pointed his giant arrow at me. What kind of a weirdo taught class with an enormous foam arrow on his hand? It was like a big yellow, pointy hand puppet. Sometimes, he even pretended the arrow would speak by answering questions for the class when they were too stupid to figure out the answers.

"May I go see my counselor?" I tried to keep my voice as low as possible. I didn't need the entire class knowing my business.

"Why? Is there a problem?" Great! The stupid arrow was talking.

For a second, I almost answered his arrow back, and then I realized I would look even more idiotic than Mr. Steinberg.

"I just really need to see her, Mr. Steinberg."

"Do you have an appointment?" The arrow pointed directly between my eyes, as if it had the power to see into my mind.

"Yes." One little white lie. I had been raised to be honest, and so far, my parents had been pretty good at ingraining that principle into my mind. *But* they never said I couldn't lie to a puppet.

"Okay."

Okay? It was that easy? If it wasn't for the psycho hall monitors on our campus, a kid could have easily gotten away with skipping class.

I reached under my desk for my binder. Summer's heels were resting on it, and I could tell by the way she held them firmly in place, she had no intention of helping me out. I yanked on my binder until I heard the banging of her heels against the metal bars. She didn't say anything, but she did give my desk one last shove before I departed.

****

Mrs. Ramirez greeted me with her pasted on smile. It wasn't like her smile was fake; she just always smiled. In my short time at Greenwood Junior High, I didn't remember Mrs. Ramirez ever having a bad day.

"How may I help you, Sophie?"

That was another incredible talent of hers; she knew every kid's name in the school. How did she do it? I couldn't even keep the names of my seven teachers straight.

"Pre-algebra is a waste of my time. I'm learning nothing." I tried to keep the whine out of my voice as I fidgeted with the creases on my binder.

"But we've just started our third week of school. If I move you to algebra, you'll be lost." Mrs. Ramirez smiled as she talked, but this wasn't her usual smile. This was the kind of smile I gave to that poor midget girl who rode my bus. Some of the immature seventh graders called her a hobbit and asked her if she'd found the ring.

"I can handle it. If I need to, I'll stay after school for tutoring. Please, Mrs. Ramirez, I can't suffer like this for a whole year." Somehow, despite my efforts, that high-pitched little whine slipped into my voice. I just couldn't help it. If I was going to change my reputation, I had to get out of bonehead math and far away from Summer Powers.

"Well, let me look at your classes." She pulled up a

screen on her computer. "We might need to change your schedule."

What? Change my schedule! No, no, she couldn't take away English. It was the only class I had with Jacob. Mrs. Ramirez was one of the few reasonable adults at this school. Surely, she wouldn't do that to me.

I tried to keep my voice calm, but I felt the shakiness in my throat. "Why? Can't I just switch first periods?"

"No." She answered quickly, without even looking from her computer. "All of the first period algebra classes are full. Let's see. Fifth period looks like the best bet."

"Fifth period?" How did I know she was going to say that? "Fifth period won't work."

Mrs. Ramirez looked up from her computer and studied me. "Why not?"

I tried not to let her see the panic in my eyes. Whatever happened, I *have* to keep my class with Jacob. "Because we are in the middle of a novel unit. I know the other English classes aren't reading Huck Finn and I'll have to catch up in English *and* in math."

"Well, I could put you in algebra if you are willing to drop your third period elective."

Third period was band, my second least favorite class. Mr. Martinelli was the kind of teacher who took pleasure in his students' misery.

Whenever he smugly smiled, folded his arms across his chest, and asked me to play, I couldn't even hold my flute steady. As I tried to control my nervousness, I inhaled sporadic puffs of air that sounded more like a dog panting than music. Mr. Martinelli told me he could lock a cat in a trash can, throw it down a flight of stairs and make better music.

"Ok. I'll drop band." I was ready to jump out of my seat. No more Summer, no more yellow arrow, and no more musical melodrama.

"So I'll have to give you a new elective first period." Mrs. Ramirez turned back to her computer and made several clicks with her mouse. "How about yearbook?"

"Yearbook?" This summer, when I reviewed my choice of electives, I hadn't even given that class a second glance. Ever since I erased that fat, ugly picture of me in my sixth grade book and replaced it with a Sponge Bob sticker, my mom told me she would never buy me a yearbook.

"I hear if you join the staff you get a free book."

"Really?" Wow! My day couldn't get much better. I'd get my own yearbook with Jacob's picture.

"Here." Mrs. Ramirez printed out a new schedule and handed it to me. "Go see Mrs. Carr. She's in room 200. She is short staffed this year. I wouldn't be surprised if she had you taking football pictures this weekend."

I had to be dreaming. Standing on the sidelines, watching Jacob Flushman and his masculine thighs as he raced toward me with the pigskin tucked under his arm. He scored a touchdown and I caught the moment with my lens. He grabbed me in excitement and planted a big kiss on my cheek. No. This was my dream. He planted a big kiss on my lips.

This schedule change was just the boost I needed. I was on my way to a fun freshman year. My confidence would grow. My life would change. So long to "So Fat" Sinora.

****

"Just what I need. Another new kid I have to train." Mrs. Carr looked down at me through thick glasses. "Do you have any photography experience?"

"No." I had wondered why this class was short staffed when students could get free yearbooks. Now I knew.

"Great." Mrs. Carr threw her hands in the air. "Do you know anything about PhotoShop?"

"No." I suddenly felt much smaller, much less significant than I had before walking through the yearbook room door.

"Terrific. There goes my first deadline." Mrs. Carr stormed off and threw herself behind her desk that was positioned in the center of the classroom. She was instantly engulfed by a huge flat-screen computer monitor on the desktop. Surrounding her desk were other computer stations, facing inward like a fortress, as if whatever was on them was top secret information.

"I can train her, Mrs. Carr." Lara "Spread 'em" Sketchum popped her head from behind one of the dozen large computer monitors.

"You're going to have to," Mrs. Carr groaned. "I'm up

to my eyeballs in paperwork. This administration doesn't think I have enough on my hands."

Lara smiled and I hesitantly smiled back. Although I'd never had Lara in a class and we hung out in entirely different circles, I knew all about her. She was the school slut. If I became friends with her, I could be labeled a slut, too. This year was my chance to prove Sophie "So Fat" was cool and making friends with Lara didn't fit in with my plan. What would Jacob think of me?

"Come sit over here, Sophie." Lara waved toward an empty seat next to hers. "I was just uploading freshmen mugshot pictures. I'll teach you how to do it, along with some of the basics of PhotoShop."

"How did you know my name?" I slipped in between a crack in the computer fortress and sat beside her.

"This is my third year on staff. I know everybody's face. Your picture has changed since seventh grade." Lara hesitantly smiled, then lowered her lashes and bit her bottom lip. *I'm not a slut. I hope you don't believe the rumors.*

Wow. I hadn't heard someone else's thoughts since before school started. Hearing her voice echo in my skull was suddenly shocking, and humbling. Lara wasn't the only student at this school who had been branded by a label.

I almost goofed and answered her thoughts. That would have been a bad thing. People would have been afraid to come near me if they knew about my gift. "Thanks, I hope my picture looks better now."

"Yeah. You lost weight; you're actually pretty."

"Thanks." Coming from Lara, that was a huge compliment. I guess whoever labeled her the school slut was jealous. With her long black hair, big blue eyes and perfect body, Lara got lots of attention from the guys.

"I'm just placing pictures of the freshmen on their pages. I'm already on the Fs." Lara must have seen my eyes widen, because she grinned after she spoke. "Do you like Jacob Flushman?"

Those traitors. Krysta and AJ blabbed their big mouths. But wait…they didn't talk Lara, which meant it must have gotten around the whole school. I wanted to die. "How did you know?"

"My lens catches everything." Lara clicked her mouse and pulled up a picture of students eating lunch.

I instantly recognized Jacob with his football buddies. They were laughing and throwing fries at each other. Then my eyes did a double take; I was sitting at the table behind Jacob and I was staring...no...drooling in his direction. Oh, how embarrassing. My mom had always told me I had an expressive face but did I have to make my crush so obvious? I felt a tinge of guilt for accusing my best friends of betraying me when my own stupid face was the culprit.

"Don't worry, your secret's safe with me." Lara gave me a reassuring smile and closed the picture.

Still stunned, I had trouble finding my voice. "Is...is that picture going in the yearbook?"

"Not if you don't want it to."

"God, no!" I accidentally screamed my answer.

Mrs. Carr looked up from her computer long enough to scowl.

Lara nudged my shoulder. "Consider it deleted."

"No, wait." No matter how embarrassing I looked, I just couldn't stand the thought of deleting Jacob.

"I'll rip you a copy first," Lara teased. "Jake does look cute in that picture."

Bad reputation or not, I knew Lara and I would become buds. A minor setback in my plan to prove to Greenwood I was cool. If Lara helped me in yearbook, the least I could do was help her uncover the myth behind the rumors. After all, if she wasn't a slut, someone was lying.

Chapter Three

Summer had to put on her makeup while I waited to get my flute out of my locker. My annoyance was overshadowed by relief; I'd never need to carry around that rusted out hunk of metal again. I was so relieved after I turned it in to Mr. Martinelli, leaving his classroom for the last time.

Between waiting for Summer and turning in my flute, I was now late to my new class. Why was I so directionally challenged? Mrs. Stein's room should have been easy to find. Two hundred. Even number. Simple. Not hardly. I was going in circles. I knew I'd seen that 'Don't be a dope' sign by the bathroom entrance at least ten times. Some idiot was smoking pot and driving into oncoming traffic. The first time, the sign made me laugh. Now I wanted to tear it down and rip it to shreds, except that wouldn't look good on my school records. They'd probably think *I* was on drugs.

"Where's your pass?" Busted. The burly voice stopped me dead in my tracks.

I turned to face my captor, a school rent-a-cop. Man—maybe. Woman—I didn't know. Big, scary mammoth beast with spiked hair—definitely.

"I...I don't have one."

"Did you think I wouldn't catch you? The bell rang five minutes ago."

How could I answer without sounding like a complete idiot? "I'm lost."

"Lost? Are you one of Mrs. Frances' kids?" The beast smiled smugly and folded its arms across its chest, obviously waiting for me to challenge the insult. Mrs. Frances' kids rode the little bus.

The list of people who liked to put me down was growing larger. I needed to stand up for myself, starting with the beast. "Mrs. Ramirez changed my schedule this

17

morning so I am still learning my new classes. I don't know where Mrs. Stein's room is." That's how I answered it. This is how I *wanted* to answer it. "No, dipstick. I may not know where I'm going, but at least everybody can tell if I wear panties or briefs."

"Let me see your schedule." The cop grabbed the twisted paper from my hands and carefully eyed the document, as if looking for a watermark or something to prove the schedule's authenticity. Because evil teenagers forge school schedules all the time. "I'm going that way now. Follow me."

I walked behind the beast, trying hard to decipher its gender. Dark roots, dyed frosted blonde at the tips, spiked with something, probably gel. Would a guy go through that much trouble to make each follicle stand up in a straight line?

Yes.

Jacob's best friend, Frankie Salas, would but then again Frankie was perfect. From his angular jaw to flawless, tanned skin and large, dark eyes, Frankie could have been ripped from the pages of *GQ*, at least that's what Krysta always said.

The beast in front of me had no butt, a large stomach, and breasts that were either big man-boobs or small girl-boobs. By the time we arrived at room two hundred, which was located in hallway three hundred—go figure—I still hadn't figured out the cop's gender. When the beast turned around, I had the chance to check the name on its badge. Tyler. No help there.

The door to Mrs. Stein's room had one window, which was covered up with butcher paper. Tyler opened the door without knocking and I noticed a teacher was writing equations on her dry-erase board.

"You have a new student."

Her arm jerked. She dropped her algebra book and her dry-erase marker at the sound of Tyler's booming voice. She turned, hand on chest and momentarily glared at Tyler before focusing her gaze on me. Her entire face softened as she beckoned me toward the front of the room. "Welcome to Algebra, dear. I'm Mrs. Stein. What's your name?"

"Sophie." I handed her my crumpled schedule.

"Sophie, how lovely." She looked at the paper before giving me a warm smile that reached her eyes. *Caryn's hair. Dark and smooth.*

How did I have two telepathic experiences in one day? And who was Caryn? I must have reminded Mrs. Stein of this person by the way she smiled.

Mrs. Stein retrieved her algebra book and clutched it to her chest. "Have a seat wherever you want. There are no assigned seats here."

I scanned the room for an empty seat. That's when I noticed the waving hand. I instantly recognized AJ, with her sporty blonde ponytail and the beat-up binder plastered with Michael Phelps pictures. I remembered her mentioning she had Mrs. Stein for algebra. "The nicest teacher in the school." Those were her exact words.

AJ had been real excited when she called me after registration this summer. Although her mom wanted her to take all honors classes, she allowed AJ the one exception with Mrs. Stein. The Mikes had Mrs. Stein. All the kids loved her.

"Hey." I sat down in an empty desk next to AJ, relieved to have a friend in class. I normally only saw her and Krysta during lunch.

"So, you finally ditched those losers in pre-algebra?" AJ smiled before we turned to the commotion at the back of the room. Tyler was trying to get to Grody Cody Miller.

Mrs. Stein was standing in front of Cody's desk, hands on hips, blocking the cop's path. "You're not taking him out of my class. If he misses one lesson, he'll be behind."

"Mr. Sparks' orders."

"I don't give a damn what Mr. Sparks said, Cody's not leaving!"

Usually students oohed and aahed when teachers swore, but not this time. They stared at her, eyes wide with something like awe. Some kids smiled. I could hear them whispering, "Go, Mrs. Stein."

I didn't get it. Grody Cody Miller was every teacher's worst nightmare. Cody had a bad attitude. He was always telling teachers off and disrupting class. Why wouldn't she have wanted him to leave?

"He left Mr. Benson's class without permission

Friday. The principal wants to see him...*now*." Tyler peered around Mrs. Stein's shoulder and narrowed its eyes at Cody.

"So that makes a whole lot of sense. Take him out of one class for leaving another. He's not going. If Sparks has a problem with it, tell him to come see me during my planning period."

"But..."

"But nothing, Tyler. I've got to teach my kids. Please leave my classroom...*now*." *You're not laying a finger on any of my babies.*

Mrs. Stein was passionate about her kids. She made that perfectly clear with her internal thoughts. When a person was extremely upset or angry, their thoughts were more likely to jump into my head. So, she thought of us as her babies? That was kind of cool, especially after coming from Mrs. Carr's class.

Tyler finally left the room, slamming the door.

Mrs. Stein faced the door, back and shoulders rigidly frozen for what seemed an eternity. She inhaled a large breath and let it out before turning to the class.

AJ started the first clap and we all followed by rising to give Mrs. Stein a standing ovation. She deserved it for the way she stood up to that scary beast. That's when I decided when I grow up, I want to be just like Mrs. Stein.

****

Fourth period was a blur. I didn't focus on science Nazi because I was too busy thinking about Jacob and his masculine thighs. Besides, I was better off ignoring a teacher like Mr. Benson. If students asked too many questions, he had panic attacks and made us stand outside the classroom, as if we were deliberately slowing down his perfectly laid out lesson plans.

I remembered the incident Friday when Grody Cody raised his hand in the middle of a lesson and asked Mr. Benson to explain how a cell divided. "Does it have a brain? How does it divide if no one tells it to? If I was a cell, I'd just sit there."

I could see the veins popping out of Mr. Benson's neck. His response—he made Cody wait outside the door. I guess Cody was tired of waiting to be invited back in, so he left.

After the bell rang to release us from our torture, I couldn't get to my fifth period class fast enough.

Crap. I left Huck Finn in my locker.

Not Huck the boy, Huck the book. We were assigned fifty pages to read over the weekend. Normally, Mrs. Warren didn't assign weekend homework, but Frankie Salas was late to class, resulting in a homework assignment for all of us. That was her policy. If one kid screwed up, we all suffered. It was usually a pretty good deterrent for tardies.

Not this time.

Although everybody was mad at Frankie for flirting too long in the hallway, we mostly kept our opinions to ourselves. As the most popular boy in school, Frankie could get away with ruining our weekend.

Passing time was only six minutes long. I rushed to my locker on the other end of the world, intending to grab the book and make the trek back to English on the other side of campus.

Not happening. Summer was at her locker, admiring her cheap Britney Spears imitation hairdo. As usual, her locker door was open flat against mine, so she could get the best view of her face in the locker mirror.

Step one to a new image. Learn to speak up for yourself.

"Excuse me."

Summer didn't pause in her makeup ritual to look in my direction. Apparently, I wasn't even as worthy as a Maybelline smudge stick.

Maybe I wasn't loud enough. "Excuse me!"

Summer opened up her lipliner and stared thoughtfully into the pen, as if she and the cosmetic were the only two things on Earth. "Hmmm. Too pink for fall. I need something darker."

"I *need* to get into my locker." I tapped my foot to make her aware of my impatience. Although, I knew she really didn't care.

"Did you hear something, Britney?" Summer spoke to her Britney Spears poster, which was taped just below her mirror. "I didn't think so."

"Hey, what are you doing on this side of the world? Isn't your next class in the one hundred hall?"

I turned to see AJ. "I'm waiting to get into my locker." I pointed at Summer, who was still consumed with wasting my time.

"That's easy to fix." AJ moved me aside and yanked Summer's lipliner out of her hands. She threw it in her locker and slammed it shut. "All clear." AJ faced Summer, narrowing her eyes in a challenging gesture.

Summer moaned, rolled her eyes and walked away.

AJ had the courage to stand up to anybody. How did she do it? Wasn't she afraid of getting her butt kicked? Sure, AJ was tough—a lot tougher than me. All her life, AJ had dealt with bullying from the Mikes making her used to fending for herself.

But AJ had a secret, other than her visions, that could be devastating if the wrong kids found out. After a horse riding accident, AJ tore the retina in her left eye. AJ's doctor said, one wrong punch, and she would lose sight in that eye forever. Even so, AJ wasn't afraid of a confrontation.

Summer was *my* problem. I couldn't risk my best friend's eyesight because I was too chicken to handle a bullying brat. "Hey, this is my problem, not yours."

"You're welcome." AJ looked at me with a smirk.

"I don't want you getting hurt over me."

AJ shook her head and snickered. "When are you going to learn to stand up for yourself? Summer wouldn't do anything to risk smudging her lipstick. For someone who can read people, you really can't *read* people."

"I mean it, AJ." Before I could finish my lame argument, I was interrupted by the sound of the tardy bell. "Oh, God!"

I ran to my fifth period class. Although, what was the use? I was tardy now. What kind of punishment had I brought down on my English class? Pop quiz, essay?

Jacob was going to hate me.

****

Opening the door to room five-o-five, Freshman English, I slid in quietly and scurried to my seat at the far side of the room. Although I didn't see Mrs. Warren, I could hear her movement from behind a big pile of books that sat atop her desk. Maybe she hadn't taken roll yet. I received only a few evil glares as my fellow classmates caught me sneaking in late, but they didn't dog me. They didn't want extra homework, either.

"You're late, Sophie!" Frankie Salas, who sat directly across from me, announced this to the entire class.

I felt every muscle in my body tense.

Frankie turned to me with a grin.

I couldn't speak, couldn't move, couldn't unstiffen my frozen face if I tried. All I could do was stare at my tormentor and think, "Why?"

"Wh...what was that? Someone came in late?" The teacher's balding head popped up from behind a pile of books in the corner of the room. It took a moment to register it wasn't Mrs. Warren talking.

Substitute teacher, Mr. Dallin, or as we so fondly called him, Mr. Pick-N-Flick, had been teaching since the beginning of time and he hadn't earned his booger picking reputation for no reason. He was my oldest sister's math teacher. She told me he left crusties on her papers at least once a week. He was our sub for three weeks in my seventh grade geography class. On two occasions, I'd caught him digging for buried treasure. He was one reason I carried antibacterial hand lotion in my backpack.

Another one of Dallin's shortcomings, he had blessedly horrible hearing and eyesight.

My lucky day.

"No, no, Mr. Dallin. I said you look great, Sophie." Frankie winked. "Doesn't she look great, Mr. Dallin?"

I felt the heat rise from my chest into my cheeks.

"I can't tell. Let me get a closer look." Mr. Dallin heaved his huge frame upward, knocking over several books in the process. He waddled his way toward me. "Sophie? Sophie Sinora, is that you?"

"Yes, Mr. Dallin."

Mr. Dallin pushed the rim of his glasses higher on his rounded nose. "You've lost some weight."

"Yes, sir." I sank lower into my seat. Every eye in the classroom was on me. I didn't need them staring at my big lips or my messed up hair. I just wanted to disappear.

"You know." He folded his arms across his chest and dazed into space. Not uncommon for Mr. Dallin. "I taught your sisters in high school."

"They told me." Great. Please go back to your books,

Mr. Dallin.

"Very popular and pretty. Wasn't your oldest sister Homecoming Queen?"

"Yes." Actually, they both were but I wasn't about to remind him. I had hoped that after a year's absence, my family legacy would be forgotten. Being the only fat dork in a line of beauty queens wasn't easy.

"That's right. Very popular and pretty."

"You just said that, sir." He was probably wondering if I was the mailman's daughter. I couldn't sink any lower, otherwise, I'd have been under the desk, so I tried to imagine I was invisible. I wasn't used to being the center of attention and having this drooling walrus hovering over me made me sick to my stomach.

"Well, Frankie, Sophie is turning into quite a beauty herself. In a couple years time, she could be the next Homecoming queen. I'd keep my eyes on this girl if I were you."

"Maybe I will," Frankie said evenly.

As expected, students snickered at this last comment while Frankie had the nerve to smile.

What a jerk. Pretending to like me. I glared at him out of the corners of my eyes.

Why would the most gorgeous guy in school play these games? What was in it for him? Did he want me to do his homework or was he just trying to add me to his long list of pathetic groupies?

Not wanting to know the answer, I fought not letting a sigh escape and faced forward, pretending to ignore Frankie. Besides, Frankie was way out of my league. I'd never expect to go out with someone as gorgeous as him, so why dream about it? Jacob was in my league, but he was the only one who didn't turn around when Mr. Dallin had the rest of the class staring at me. He didn't even laugh when Frankie was flirting.

I wondered why.

This could have been a good sign, but it could also have been very bad. I wished I could have popped into his head. All my intuition failed me, and, as usual, my gift was stubborn. I had to satisfy my curiosity by simply staring at his perfectly small ears, buzz cut dark hair and thick neck.

Suddenly, Jacob jerked hard in his seat. "Come on. Come on. Yes!" The excitement in his voice held back in a whisper.

I couldn't believe it. Jacob could have cared less about me. He was too busy playing his Game Boy. Frankie and I could have made out on top of his desk and I don't think he would have noticed.

Mr. Dallin began speaking above the din of the noisy classroom. "Ok, everyone, your teacher will be out for the next six weeks."

As was always the case when we had a substitute teacher, there were no rules for classroom behavior. The class stopped talking long enough to exchange high fives and cheers. Nobody asked what happened to Mrs. Warren. Nobody cared.

"Her daughter is having a baby."

Mr. Dallin could have been speaking to empty desks. After the gone-for-six-weeks part, the students didn't want to listen to anything else he had to say.

And neither did I. I had more important things to worry about. Why didn't Jacob notice me? Even blind Mr. Dallin thought I was getting pretty.

Wham!

The classroom stilled as our attention was riveted on Mr. Dallin at the front of the room. He held the yardstick he'd just slammed across Grody Cody's desk. Cody looked ready to piss his pants.

"Now, do I have your attention?"

Some of us silently nodded, but mostly we just stared.

"Have I finished collecting all copies of Huck Finn or are there any still missing?" He scanned the room.

I swallowed hard. Huck was still in my backpack. I tentatively raised my hand.

"Pass it up, Sophie."

I unzipped my bag with shaky fingers, accidentally dumping the contents on the floor. Why was I so nervous? This was Pick-N-Flick. He'd never beat his students before, at least not that I'd heard.

I tried to hand my book to Jacob, but he didn't turn around. He was so busy getting his butt kicked by a video game, he wasn't paying attention to what was going on in the real world.

"Jacob." I leaned forwarded and whispered, inhaling a mixed scent of hair gel and a strong, rich musk. But there was something else. Could it have been ketchup? I decided hair gel, musk and ketchup were the perfect odors for a guy.

"Jacob." I whispered louder. For days I'd been dreaming of the moment I'd get so close to Jacob I could almost kiss him. Here I was, asking him to take my book, and the moron wasn't even listening. "Jacob, Mr. Dallin is watching us. Take the book."

Nothing.

"Jacob!" Mr. Dallin's yardstick slammed down across Jacob's desk, casing him to drop his Game Boy.

"What the hell!" Jacob puffed up his chest and looked ready to jump out of his desk and punch Dallin.

Jacob was going to get himself in trouble and my Huck Finn was the cause of it.

"Jake, chill." Frankie leaned out of his desk and picked up Jacob's Game Boy. He placed it in Dallin's outstretched hand.

"That's mine." Jacob shot an angry glance at Frankie and then at Dallin.

"Not anymore." Dallin took both the Game Boy and my Huck Finn and walked to the front of the room. He slid the Game Boy in the top drawer of Mrs. Warren's desk and put my book on top of the already large stack of books on the desktop. "Now that I have all the books collected, get out a pencil for a pop quiz on chapter six."

"This sucks!"

Jacob really needed to shut up. It was just a toy. If he kept it up, he could get suspended and miss a *real* game, his football game on Friday.

Jacob slammed his fists on his desk. "I don't want Pick-N-Flick getting crusties on my game."

Mr. Dallin narrowed his eyes at Jacob, his fat cheeks swelled, looking like balloons ready to burst. He pointed toward the door and screamed at Jacob. "Get out!"

Jacob stormed out and slammed the door.

Mr. Dallin would probably send a referral to the office. Jacob would miss his next football game, maybe even be suspended from the team. This was all my fault.

If I hadn't forgotten Huck. If I had stood up to Summer. If I hadn't been late.

"Sophie, can you take this to the office for me?" Dallin handed me a large, brown office envelope and an orange hall pass.

Why me?

I knew what was in the envelope—Jacob's referral. I felt as if all eyes in the class were upon me. I had two choices—throw it away and pray Dallin's ancient memory would forget the incident or seal Jacob's doom by delivering the referral. Either way I was screwed. Could my life get any worse?

****

Five minutes. That's all I needed to drop off a referral at the office and return to class. Ten minutes if I stretched it out some, walked slowly, took a potty break. Dallin wouldn't have missed me. I had noticed he'd forgotten to write a time on my hall pass. This gave me some time to decide what to do.

I had always considered myself a good kid. Besides, I valued my weekends too much to get in trouble. I was thinking how easy it would have been to find the nearest bathroom and stuff the referral in the garbage. I had to wonder, though, was Jacob worth the risk? Would Jacob do something like this for me? Jacob didn't even know I existed. He proved that when he ignored me over his Game Boy.

"Sophie!" Caught up in my worries, I didn't even notice Jacob standing by the boys' bathroom.

"Hey." I was such an idiot. The man of my dreams finally acknowledged my existence, he even knew my name, and all I could manage was 'hey'. I put my right hand behind my back, hiding Jacob's referral.

"Did you get kicked out, too?" His dark grey eyes simmered with anger, his lips drawn in a tight line. Suddenly, I realized his pissed off expression was kind of hot.

Stay focused.

"No." How did I tell him I was about to make his day worse?

His eyes narrowed. "Where are you going?"

I tried to recall one of the many pieces of wisdom my

parents crammed down my throat. Honesty is always best. "To the office."

Jacob closed the distance until we were frightfully only a few feet apart. His nearness set off unfamiliar sparks of energy. My stomach began to twist in knots and I felt my entire body quaking inside.

He peered around my shoulder. "What's in the envelope?"

"I...I don't know." And honestly I didn't; although I suspected, as Jake probably did, that it was his referral.

Jacob moved closer. "You don't know?" His eyebrows rose.

His question felt more like an accusation. I was sure Jacob could hear my heart pounding. His nearness was about to shatter my nerves into a million pieces. I tried my best to regain composure. "Probably your referral."

"Yeah. I guess I lost my cool." He cast his eyes downward, his long, black lashes fluttered across his squeezable cheeks. "My dad's going to kick my ass when he finds out."

"Maybe he won't find out." I should have kept my mouth shut. That sounded like a promise and I was still unsure of what to do.

"He's friends with Sparks. He'll find out and I'll be grounded for a month." Jacob put his hands in his pockets and kept his gaze down before turning his large puppy dog eyes back to me.

How could I resist Jacob? He was so cute and sweet. "Well, what do you want me to do?" The pounding in my chest rose to my throat.

The corners of his mouth turned up slightly. "Maybe you could give that referral to me."

I couldn't still my shaking limbs. "And then what?"

"Dallin probably forgot about it already." Jacob reached around my back and grabbed my hand. I jerked, surprised by the tingling sensation of his skin touching my overly sensitive fingers. His nearness and the scent of musky ketchup was almost my undoing.

Oh, God, I could have died happy.

"Yeah. You're right." I gulped as I felt him gently pry the envelope from my hand. "But what if he doesn't?"

Jacob raised one edge of his mouth and flashed a

lopsided grin. "Come on?" He already had the envelope opened and was scanning the document.

He fisted the paper into a ball and tossed it in a nearby trashcan. "Thanks. You know, Dallin is right. You have changed."

I jerked my head, trying to digest what he'd just said. He *was* paying attention when Dallin and Frankie were talking about me. Could this mean he was interested in me?

Before I could stop him, as if I would want to stop him, Jacob planted a kiss on my cheek. Although it was just a quick peck, that kiss lingered on my skin for an eternity. If it wasn't for personal hygiene, I would have never washed my face.

"See you later, Sophie."

I loved the way Jacob said my name, like chocolate pudding rolling off his tongue.

Jacob walked down the hall, leaving me standing there, stroking my cheek and contemplating his words, his kiss.

You have changed. What did that mean? Did he think I was cool? Pretty? His statement had endless possibilities. AJ and Krysta had to help me decipher his meaning on the bus ride home.

****

I sighed as I dreamily watched the cars pass by my window. He kissed me. He said I changed. "I wonder if it's time?" I said to no one in particular as I wondered aloud. A girl in love was aloud to wonder.

"Time for what?" Krysta asked in a disinterested voice while her nose was buried in a *Cosmo* article.

"Time to ask him to Freshmen Formal." I twisted my fingers and swished my feet. Nothing could burst this bubble.

"I think it's time for you to get a life." AJ's smug expression taunted me from behind her seat.

Stunned, I looked at her. "What's that supposed to mean?"

"Sits the bench." AJ held up her fingers and began a countdown. "Game Boy in class, referral, what's next?"

I rolled my eyes. "He had a bad day."

"No, he *created* a bad day." AJ leaned forward. "I

think it's time for a new crush, Sophie."

"I'm not in the mood for this, AJ." Crossing my arms, I turned sideways.

AJ leaned closer. "Not in the mood for the truth?"

I turned back, coming within inches of her face. "Drop it, AJ."

"Fine." She slouched back in her seat and covered her face with her hands.

AJ wasn't the type to give up so easily. Something wasn't right.

"What's wrong, AJ?" I asked.

She peered at me through a slit in her fingers. "I fell asleep in Spanish."

Krysta flipped the page of her *Cosmo* before looking up. "Mess up your makeup?"

"No," AJ sneered. "I had a bad dream."

"What was it about?" I could feel my goose bumps rise. Whenever AJ had a dream, something bad happened.

AJ's voice faltered. "I'm afraid to talk about it."

"Why?" I already knew the answer. The tiny hairs on my skin stood on end, as I tried to rub the chill out of my arms.

AJ shrugged before looking out the window. "It might come true."

Krysta quirked a brow and set down her magazine, trying to keep her voice to a whisper. "Was this a dream or a vision?"

Recognizing the seriousness of the situation, I moved closer and Krysta followed.

AJ turned back toward us, her eyes glossed over with moisture. "Someone is going to die," AJ whispered. "I didn't see who it was, but I think it's someone close to us."

Krysta's eyes bulged, her jaw stiffened. "Are you sure?"

"Yeah." A single tear slipped down AJ's cheek.

This wasn't happening. My entire body tingled with numbness. Fear took hold of me so tightly, I felt as if I would shatter into a million pieces. Was it me, was it my mom? "You didn't get a look?"

"It's someone old. I saw white hair."

I sighed, slightly relieved. "All my grandparents are

dead."

"My grandpa is dead, but not my grandma." AJ gripped the back of her seat so tightly, her knuckles turned white.

Krysta squeezed her hand. "Maybe it was just a dream."

"Yeah." AJ's voice turned to stone. "Maybe."

****

Someone turn down that music. I'm trying to sleep here. Wait a minute. Is that my phone?

I rolled out of bed and fumbled through my dirty clothes strewn on the floor. Somewhere among the rubble was my cell phone. I had to turn off that stupid song before the noise woke my parents. AJ changed my settings again and downloaded Michael Jackson. Not funny. Her mom wouldn't buy her a cell, so she was always messing with mine.

I finally found my little lime green phone and flipped it open. Incoming call, Krysta, 1:30 am. Something was wrong.

I hit talk. "Krysta, what is it?"

I could hear muffled sobs in the background. "She's dead."

"Who's dead?"

After a long pause, Krysta whispered her answer. "Grammy."

I felt the tightness in my throat, tears threatening to escape my eyes. "Oh, no...not Grammy."

Although Grammy wasn't related to Krysta, she'd been her neighbor for most of Krysta's life, up until Krysta's mom left and her dad lost the mortgage on house. But even after that, Grammy visited Krysta's apartment at least once a week, bringing her cookies and home-cooked meals. She was the closest thing to a grandma Krysta ever had.

Krysta hiccupped and continued crying.

I sat there for a few moments, letting her get some tears out before asking another question. "How, Krysta?"

"I...I don't know how."

Then I knew. Krysta had a supernatural visit. Spooky. Chills of fear swept over my neck and down my spine. "When did she come see you?"

31

"Tonight."

"What did she say?" Although I was terrified, I still wanted to know the answer.

"She's not saying anything."

I dropped the phone, hastily picking it back up and accidentally pressing a few buttons while I tried to control my shaky fingers. "She's...she's still there?"

Krysta sniffed once before answering. "Uh-huh."

My mom had always told me it was impolite to talk on the phone when you had visitors. I wondered what she would have said in this situation. Even though Grammy was nice, I'd still freak if a dead person came for a visit. Krysta needed me so I tried to think of the right thing to say, but my brain was numb from terror. Clearing my throat, words finally found their way out of my mouth. "Do you think she likes you talking on the phone?"

"I don't know. She won't speak to me."

Creepy. Krysta must have been so weirded out. "What's she doing?"

"Sitting at the foot of my bed."

"Where are you?"

I felt the fear in Krysta's voice. "In bed."

Oh, God.

On bad days when I felt cursed with my gift, all I had to do was remember poor Krysta. How did she manage to stay sane? Krysta needed my help, but I wasn't familiar with handling spirits. "So what do you want me to do?"

"Just talk to me until she goes away."

I felt Krysta's pain as if I was living inside Krysta's body. The agony of losing Grammy clenched my chest and then a spasm of guilt washed over me. *I'm sorry, Grammy.* I knew from her thoughts, Krysta didn't want to hurt Grammy's feelings, but she was also terrified.

"This is your last chance to talk to her before she's gone forever, Krysta."

"But she's been sitting here for over three hours."

I closed my eyes and tried to sense Grammy's thoughts, but I couldn't feel the turmoil I sensed in Krysta. Then the warmth washed over me; I heard Grammy's voice. *Peace.*

"I think she wants peace."

"Peace," Krysta sniffled, "how do you know?"

"I just listened to her thoughts." Completely amazed at what I just said, it was as if someone else was talking for me. Then it hit me; good, God, how did I just hear the thoughts of a dead person?

"Are you sure?" The tone in Krysta's voice changed to disbelief. "I didn't think you could control your mind reading."

"I can't, normally. I can't explain why I can do it now, but trust me, Krysta, she wants peace."

"How do I give her that?"

I closed my eyes and tried again to channel Grammy's thoughts through the phone. *Krysta at peace.*

Before I could hear anything more from Grammy, Krysta interrupted my thoughts. "Sophie." Krysta let out a sob, the feeling of her guilt surged through me again. "This isn't how I want to remember Grammy."

"Try going back to sleep," I suggested.

"Are you crazy?"

I knew Krysta wouldn't like that idea. Then again, I couldn't blame her. Just imagining a dead person staring at me while I slept, my entire body numbed with terror.

"She just wants to see you at peace before she departs. I think she wants to know you'll be okay without her."

"So you want me to go to sleep?" I heard the uncertainty in Krysta's quivering voice.

"Yeah." I reassured her. "But first maybe you should say goodbye."

"Bye, Gram. I love you," Krysta choked.

Knowing this would be the last time Krysta would see her Grammy, tears stung my eyes as I swallowed a lump in my throat. "Okay, now lay down. Keep the phone on. I won't hang up, I promise."

Krysta hesitated before consenting. "Okay."

I heard Krysta snoring about a half hour later. By this time there was no way I could sleep. I was sitting straight up in bed, lights on, trying to get over the shock. How was I able to control my gift? Would I be able to control mind reading from now on? Or was this just a fluke? Why was I able to use it on a dead person? A dead person! The fright from that encounter was still setting in. Until tonight, never, ever, had I read the thoughts of a ghost.

Chapter Four

Although AJ and I shared the same bus stop, Krysta's stop was two miles before ours. The next morning, I had barely enough time to explain Grammy's visit to AJ before we got on the bus.

Krysta looked at us through swollen lids. "They found Grammy this morning."

"Where was she?" I grabbed Krysta's hand and squeezed it for comfort.

"My old neighbor saw her in the backyard, lying in her flower garden, and called my dad." Krysta put her head down, letting a few tears slip.

AJ faced us from her front perch. "What happened?"

Krysta kept her eyes focused on her lap. "They think it was a heart attack."

"I'm so sorry, Krysta." I reached for a tissue out of my backpack and handed it to her.

"Thanks." Krysta dabbed her eyes with the tissue. "At least I was able to cry this morning without my dad asking questions."

I watched as Krysta quickly soaked the tissue, and I handed her another. "Will there be a funeral?"

"I don't know. Grammy doesn't have any family." Krysta nearly choked on her last words as she turned from us, staring out the bus window.

I put my arm around Krysta's shoulders. She fell into my arms and cried the rest of the way to school.

As soon as we got off the bus, Krysta reached into her purse for her mirror. She gasped when she noticed her reflection. "I need to go to the bathroom. I can't go around looking like this."

"I'll go with you. Do you need to get to your locker before Summer gets there, Sophie?" AJ smiled accusingly.

"Yeah." I was ashamed my best friend knew I was chicken. I was tired from last night and I just wasn't in the mood to deal with Summer's crap today. I didn't like leaving Krysta, but AJ would be with her.

Just as I had hoped, Summer wasn't there yet and I was able to grab all the books I needed for my first through fifth period classes. Sure, backpacking fifty pounds of books was a pain, but not having to risk bumping into Summer was worth the extra tonnage. At least, that's what I kept telling myself.

Now I had fifteen minutes until the first bell rang and I couldn't walk the campus for that long lugging algebra, history and science books. I'd look like one of those brainy dorks. I opted for getting to my first period early. Maybe I could take a ten minute power nap at my desk. My limbs were numbing and my eyelids felt like dead weights. Obviously a side effect of last night's ghostly encounter.

I used my elbow on the door handle of the yearbook room to pry it open. The room was quiet and I didn't see anyone stirring. I could slip in and out in seconds. Out of the corner of my eye, I saw a feminine figure rush past me. I turned to see a slim hand grasping a circular door. The door rotated, engulfing the shadowy figure until she disappeared. The door turned loudly until it made a full circle. The space in the center where the girl had stood was empty.

Had Lara not told me about the darkroom yesterday, I would have been mystified by the girl's disappearance. The darkroom, Lara said, was only used for fun now, as digital equipment replaced developing pictures. Still, she told me when we were finished with our deadlines she would teach me how to develop film. I couldn't wait to hang pictures up to dry like they did in the old movies. For right now, though, I wanted to see what was behind that circular door.

Walking up to the entrance, I couldn't miss the sign. "No entrance without permission." Well, I kind of had permission. Lara said she'd teach me. I was on staff, but Mrs. Carr had never given me permission. I thought about asking her. I would have hated to be on her bad side any more than I already was.

Come on, Sophie, make up your mind. Ok, leave, and ask Lara to show you later.

Decision made, I was about to turn when I heard the faint sounds of a girl crying.

Damn. I can't leave now. She might need me. Besides, helping someone in distress would give me a good excuse to see what's behind the door.

I stepped inside, not knowing exactly what to do. I'd been in department stores with circular doors before, but with those doors I could always see what was on the other side.

How hard could it be? Just grab the handle and turn. Within seconds, everything was dark. Pure dark, except for a faint light at the end of a pitch black tunnel. I hesitantly stepped out of the doorway, tripping over the bottom runner of the door. I reached into pure blackness, hoping to steady myself, and screamed when I found nothing to hold onto.

"Who's there?" The voice echoed at the end of the room.

I managed to grab onto the smooth surface of a wall without falling. "Me."

"Okay. *Me* doesn't help me at all."

Although we hadn't been friends long, I was pretty sure the voice belonged to Lara. "It's Sophie." Slowly, I inched my way toward her voice. I wasn't sure, but I thought I heard the sound of running water.

"Sophie, what are you doing in here?" By her agitated tone, she didn't sound too happy that I had interrupted her privacy.

I tried to make out her form in the blackness, but I realized the faint light I had seen earlier was just a thin strip at the bottom of my feet. There had to be a door separating us. "I heard someone crying."

"I wasn't crying." Although I hadn't identified that 'someone' as Lara, she was quick to deny she had been sobbing. A sure sign of guilt.

I was closer to the door now and I had my proof when I heard her sniffle. "Yes, you were, Lara. I can still hear it in your voice."

"It's nothing," she breathed out. "I'm fine."

"No, you're not. Open the door, Lara." I moved my hands across the smooth surface, trying to locate the handle.

"I don't want to talk about it," she insisted.

But she did. She needed to talk to someone. I *knew* it. Maybe I could just listen to her thoughts. I closed my eyes, trying to summon my gift as I had done last night. *You can't help me. No one can help me.*

"Maybe I can." Before I realized it, I was answering her thoughts aloud.

"What?"

"I…I said maybe you can talk about it." Good save, Sophie. I gave myself a mental pat on the back for catching my 'oops' in time. I closed my eyes, willing my mind to hear what Lara was thinking.

Everyone at this school thinks I'm a slut thanks to Summer Powers, and if you knew what Jacob just said to me, I don't think you'd like him very much.

I could feel a knot forming in the pit of my stomach. "What?" She couldn't have just thought anything bad about Jacob.

"I didn't say anything," Lara blurted. "You shouldn't be in here. You haven't been trained yet."

"I'm not leaving. Tell me what's wrong." If Jacob was a creep, I had a right to know. But did I want to know?

"I already told you *nothing's* wrong!"

Lara wasn't ready to talk about her problem with me. That was understandable. We'd just become friends. I needed to get Lara to trust me. This sucked, because I knew once she told me, I might not like what I heard. Then again, maybe she was wrong about Jacob or maybe she misunderstood what he said.

"Look, I'm sorry for getting mad at you." The tone in Lara's voice softened. "Some guy on the bus called me a slut. You know, the usual."

"But you're not a slut." Jacob couldn't have been 'some guy'. I wouldn't believe it. She wasn't hearing correctly. Or maybe it was someone who sounded like Jacob.

I heard the door open a crack and Lara's hand found mine. "Thanks for not believing the rumors." She pulled me into a small room with red lights on the ceiling. I noticed a large sink. Inside the sink was a faucet that was connected to a tube that ran water into a large basin. Beside the basin were three trays with a different color liquid in each.

Just like the movies.

"Whoa. This is cool."

Lara grabbed something that looked like my mom's salad tongs and used them to lift a picture of a puppy out of the water. She shook off the picture and hung it on what looked like a clothesline. "Do you want to see some pictures I developed?"

"Yeah." The darkroom made me forget about Lara's problem. The water, the lights, it was so...peaceful. "But wait, is there something else you want to tell me?"

"No. That's it. It's over. Do you want to see these pictures or not?"

"Yeah, I want to see them." I sighed in relief. I really didn't want to hear what else Lara had to say. Jacob was a sweetie. Wasn't he? An uncomfortable, sinking feeling, grabbed hold of my chest. Was it guilt? Lara was so thankful I didn't believe in the rumors, but I refused to believe her when it came to Jacob. Maybe Jacob did call her a slut. Maybe he was just having a bad day. Jacob was too cute and perfect to be a jerk all the time.

Chapter Five

Eeeww. I shouldn't have asked for cheese on my burger. I shouldn't have asked for *burger* on my burger. I tried to digest the processed cardboard the lunch ladies thought to pass off as meat, but I just wasn't in the mood to eat. Not with the weight of the world on my shoulders.

"Do I need to kick her ass for you?"

"What?" I looked up to see AJ. I hadn't even noticed she was sitting across from me, trying to chew through a piece of leathery burger.

AJ's face twisted with disgust as she swallowed what she had chewed. "You look upset. Is Summer bothering you again or are you still freaked out about the ghost?"

"Neither." I turned my attention toward my soda. At least that was digestible, even if it was 150 calories and loaded with caffeine.

"Oh, I get it." AJ leaned back and smiled in the direction of the jock table.

Until that very moment, I hadn't even noticed them. Jacob and a couple other jocks were smashing ketchup packets, making a mess all over the white cafeteria walls.

I sighed. "He's part of it, but not all of it."

AJ arched her brow in disbelief. "Well, what's the rest?"

"I'm getting better at it." I focused on my drink again, trying to keep my voice low while speaking around my straw.

"At what?"

I hesitated, and looked around to see if anyone at the nearby tables was paying attention. "At controlling *it*."

"Oh, really," AJ smiled. "What am I thinking?"

"Don't be a dork. First Grammy, and then..." Lara had not asked me to keep it a secret; then again, she didn't know I knew.

AJ leaned closer. "Finish."

I covered my mouth while I whispered my top secret information to AJ. Just because kids weren't in hearing distance, didn't mean none of them were good lip readers. "A girl in one of my classes is having problems."

AJ's eyes widened. "What kind of problems?"

"I don't want to talk about it. She probably doesn't want anyone to know."

"What did she say?"

AJ wasn't going to let this one drop easily.

"She wouldn't tell me anything. I heard her crying, so I listened to her thoughts."

"Great." AJ backed away and narrowed her icy blue eyes at me. "So now you're using *it* to be nosey."

I tried to keep my voice low. I didn't want to cause a scene. "No, I'm not."

"Sounds like it to me." AJ threw the remnants of her burger into the wrapper and fisted it into a ball.

I looked over my shoulder, quickly scanning the room for any eavesdroppers. "What's your problem, AJ?"

"I don't know." AJ raised her voice. "Why don't you pop into my head and find out?"

I could feel my body shudder in fear that I would be found out. When we revealed our gifts to each other six years ago, we made a promise to secrecy and AJ was about to blow it with her big mouth. "Don't be a jerk, AJ."

"What are you two fighting about?" Krysta took a seat next to AJ with her usual lunch, a diet Coke and a Slim Fast bar. As if *she* needed to diet; she was skinnier than a toothpick.

AJ turned to Krysta and pointed a finger. She made no attempt to control her loud voice. "Sophie's figured out how to pry into other people's business."

"Would you keep your voice down?" I hissed, "I wanted to help."

"So, how'd you help her?" AJ snapped.

I took a deep breath, preparing for AJ to pounce again. "I don't know how to help her."

AJ slammed her fist on the table. "Just don't try any of that crap on me because I'll know when you're doing it."

I jerked back, surprised by the loud sound and AJ's reaction. "I didn't plan on it, AJ."

"Okay, you two." Krysta jumped in with an angry

whisper. She nodded toward a bunch of middle school maggots who had stopped chewing their meat products long enough to gawk at us. Kids at this school loved fights, especially little seventh graders. "Stop fighting."

"I didn't start it." I pointed to AJ and rolled my eyes for emphasis.

AJ got up and threw away her lunch. She didn't even bother to say goodbye as she stormed out the door.

"What's up with her?" I asked Krysta. After what I'd been through with Grammy and Lara, I really didn't need AJ adding to my stress.

"She had another fight with her mom last night." Krysta said this with little emotion, as if she was used to AJ and her mom fighting.

AJ had me so pissed off with her attitude, my heart was beating like a drum in my chest, and I could feel red hot anger flush into my cheeks. "Well, she doesn't have to take it out on me."

I knew AJ and her mom fought a lot. Which was why she was grounded almost every weekend, although usually just on Fridays. She would drive her mom so crazy by Saturday morning, Mrs. Dawson would give in, just to get AJ off her back.

Krysta smiled weakly and set down her diet soda. "I never got to thank you for what you did for me and Grammy."

"No problem." Although Krysta was a master at changing the subject to avoid conflict, the reminder of her loss brought on a surge of guilt. I was ashamed I was too busy being mad at AJ to remember Krysta had just lost her Grammy. "How are you holding up?"

"Ok, right now. Ask me again in a few minutes." Krysta lowered her voice to a whisper. "So, are you really learning to control it? I thought last night was just a fluke."

I looked up to see a few of the seventh graders still staring. I growled at them, and they quickly turned, frantically shoveling fries into their faces.

Leaning toward Krysta, I decided to tell her what I'd just told AJ. I knew she'd be more understanding. "I did, too. Now, I don't know. This past week thoughts have been coming more frequently. Last night with Grammy and again this morning, all I had to do was think about it."

"Who were you trying to help?" She nibbled on her diet bar and raised her gaze in anticipation.

"I don't want to say. Someone at school has started rumors about her and now other kids are teasing her." I didn't mention there was only one 'other kid', Jacob Flushman. I still didn't have proof he was that much of a jerk. "Let's just leave it at that."

Krysta took a dainty sip of her diet drink from a straw. "Are you going to help her?"

"I don't know what to do." I breathed out and rested my forehead on my palms. This day hadn't started out well and it wasn't getting any better. "I don't know how to help her, but I've got to think of something."

What could I do to help Lara? Since I had pried into her mind without permission, now was it my responsibility to help her? What could *I* do? Kick Summer's butt? Doubtful. Tell off Jacob? Then he'd never like me. But if I knew he treated my friends like crap, would I want him to like me? My life was way too complicated.

Chapter Six

Pop quiz.

Two of the most dreaded words in a student's vocabulary. Not the sight I was looking forward to when I walked into English class. I much preferred staring at the back of Jacob's cute ears. I couldn't get the dreaded vision of Dallin's scribble out of my mind, especially since those two evil words were glaring at me in bold red marker on the white board.

Our assignment last night had been to read chapter eight. Yeah, I read it, but I didn't expect to recall any of it. My mind was too filled with other stuff right now, not to mention I could barely keep my eyelids open. My caffeine high from that jumbo Dr. Pepper I had at lunch was already starting to wear down.

Mr. Pick-N-Flick made his way to the front of the classroom and opened his mouth as if to speak, but then he began to hack and cough. God, I felt sorry for the kids in the front row. Debris was flying everywhere. Didn't the guy know how to cover his mouth? He grabbed a tissue and finally coughed up whatever was blocking his passage. I couldn't see it behind the tissue, but I could hear it and it sounded slimy. The kids in the front row were turning green. Good thing I didn't eat that hamburger. I already wanted to hurl my soda.

Pick-N-Flick managed to spew out, "Clear your desks," and then he started hacking again. He grabbed another tissue and spit into it. When he tried to toss the tissue into the trashcan, a long trail of rubbery snot trailed from his lower lip to the tissue.

Now I really wanted to barf.

The tissue dangled from his lip for a second before it hit the floor. Pick-N-Flick picked it up and threw it away, but he managed to slime his hand in the process. I watched him wipe it on his pants before he grabbed the tests off his desk.

"Sophie, would you hand these out for me?"

How did I know that was coming? No telling how many boogery germs were on those tests. All eyes in the classroom were on me. Even if I doused myself with an entire bottle of antibacterial lotion, nothing would sanitize the stigma of being labeled the girl who rubbed her hands in Pick-N-Flick snot.

I sank lower in my seat, trying to avoid the teacher's gaze. "I feel really sick right now, Mr. Dallin."

"What's wrong?" He lowered his gaze, smirking. "Girl thing?"

Okay, if that's what you think, Dallin, I'll go for it. I placed my hand on my stomach and leaned forward in pain. "I just don't think I can get up right now."

"Jacob, get up here and hand these out."

I could see the backs of Jacob's ears turning red. He slowly turned, and narrowing his eyes he mouthed, "You owe me."

Poor Jacob. Poor me. I kept striking out with him. I frantically searched through my backpack, hoping he'd forgive me if I let him use my anti-bacterial lotion. Besides, I didn't like the idea of "The Love of My Life" encrusted in boogers.

Using the tips of his fingers, Jacob placed the test on my desk and scowled before moving on. Other girls in class were getting out their lotion and lathering up their hands as they reached for their tests.

Girls always come prepared. Guys never think of this stuff. Frankie leaned over, smiling, and pointed to the lotion I'd placed on my desk. "Hey, can I use some of that?"

"Help yourself. Do you think Jacob is mad at me?"

"Don't worry about him." He winked and handed back the bottle. "He'll get over it."

Jacob took the lotion from me when he returned. Bending over my desk, he whispered, "Don't think this gets you off the hook."

I shivered at the feel of his warm breath in my ear. The feel of him so near was frightening, yet exciting.

I had a hard time concentrating on the test, especially since I had to recall information while trying not to touch the paper. It was a difficult task. I ended up touching the test several times. By the end of the exam, I was almost out of lotion.

"Time's up. Now pass your test to the person who sits behind you. If you're in the last row, pass your paper to the front. We're grading these in class."

Aaugghh, does the torture never end? Was I to touch all of Dallin's boogers before the period was through?

As I reached for Jacob's test, he grabbed my hand, pulling me closer. Was this the moment I'd been waiting for? Was Jacob about to declare his love? I could feel the hairs on the back of my neck stand up in anticipation.

"This is a good time to pay me back. I didn't exactly read the book. An A would be nice, but I'd settle for an A minus."

Had I just heard him right? Did Jacob expect me to cheat for him? Before I had time to respond, I was ready to melt, feeling the warm pressure of Jacob's hand in mine. I looked into his big brown eyes, waiting, hoping. Then I felt the hard, slick object he placed in my hand.

"Use my pen if you need to change anything. Try not to write like a girl."

Wait a minute, I hadn't agreed to this. First, he made me throw away his referral, *now* I had to cheat for him. I wanted Jacob to like me, but I didn't like the sinking feeling in my gut, the feeling of being used.

****

"So what'd you do?" Krysta batted her eyes at me from over the top of her *Cosmo*. I couldn't see the rest of her face. She was probably using the magazine to conceal a smile.

I looked out the window, not wanting to witness my friends' reactions. "I cheated for him."

"No way!" AJ leaned into me from the seat in front of us. I could hear her ponytail flapping in the breeze from the open window. "Sophie's a baaad girl." She let out a mocking laugh.

"Shut up!" I wanted to grab her ponytail and throw her out the window, but I knew I'd probably regret it later.

"What'd you give him?" Krysta leaned forward, a slight frown knitting her brow, her voice dropping to barely audible.

"An A."

I barely whispered this, but their resounding squeals let me know they'd heard.

AJ jumped up from her seat, almost falling forward and into my lap. "What did he *really* get?"

"He missed every question."

"Sounds like a real winner." AJ sank into her seat again and rolled her eyes. "Lazy in sports, lazy in school."

I focused my gaze on her smug expression. "Just 'cause he sits the bench, doesn't make him lazy. That's the coach's decision."

"Yeah," AJ jabbed, "and the coach decided to sit Jacob because he's lazy."

"You have a serious attitude problem and I am seriously tired of it." I folded my arms across my chest. "I like Jacob, AJ, and I don't like you talking crap about him."

"Sorry, I've been on edge." AJ's shoulders slumped and she hunched over in her seat.

"Yeah," I said. "Just a little."

"You'd be too if you had a mother like mine." AJ had a point, even though she had a bad way of relieving stress.

"Let's get back to the subject, Sophie." Krysta grabbed my elbow. "Did he at least thank you for fixing his test?"

"Yeah, he thanked me."

AJ piped up again. "I think he's using you."

"I'm not stupid," I snapped at AJ. "I know I'm being used."

"Well, what are you going to do about it?" Krysta squeezed my arm again. Her big brown eyes showed genuine concern. "Are you just going to keep cheating for him?"

"No." I threw my head back and heaved a sigh.

AJ narrowed her eyes. "You're not going to pry into his mind, are you?"

"No, AJ," I hissed, "I will not use my gift to find out what other people think of me. Truthfully, I really don't want to know what other people are thinking about me, especially you right now."

"So," Krysta butted in, changing the subject. "How will you find out if he's using you?"

I smiled at Krysta. "I had Dallin two years ago as a sub. My sisters had him, too."

Krysta quirked an eyebrow. "What's that got to do with anything?"

"He gives pop quizzes every week," I explained, "and each time we either pass our tests to the front or back."

Krysta's eyes widened. "Ooohhhh yeeeahhhh. I see, now. So, next time Jacob will grade your test."

Although I didn't want Jacob to use me, I would be crushed if I discovered he had no feelings for me. Still, I had no choice but to find out. Love sucks. "I might have to get a few wrong on purpose, just to see if he'll cheat for me. The only problem is I never know which way Dallin will make us pass our tests."

Krysta scratched her head in contemplation. "What are you going to do if Jacob passes his test to you again? Will you change his grade?"

That was an option I didn't want to consider, but Krysta forced it out in the open. The nagging question would haunt me. "I don't know, Krysta. I just don't know."

Things would have been much easier for me if I didn't have a conscience. Unfortunately, when my parents raised me, they taught me honesty. I had to find out if Jacob liked me, and other than reading his mind, I saw this as the only way. The question was, after all this lying and cheating for him, would I still like myself?

Chapter Seven

"I don't get it." Looking at Mrs. Stein's dry-erase board, I rubbed my throbbing temples.

AJ threw down her pen and rolled her eyes at me. "Why don't you get it?"

"I don't *know* why." I couldn't hide the irritation in my voice. Algebra was to me what AJ's mom was to her, a nagging pain in the butt. "If I *knew* why, I'd probably get it."

"Sophie, let me see your equation." Mrs. Stein walked over, her algebra book clutched closely to her chest.

The way she carried that thing around all the time, I'd swear it was her child.

"I didn't finish it, Mrs. Stein." I hated to disappoint my favorite teacher, but I really felt like an idiot when it came to math.

"What's the matter?" Her soft, kind eyes scanned my face, and then trailed off in the direction of the scribble I'd written on the board.

"I don't get it." It didn't help I couldn't focus in class. But how could I? Lately, Mrs. Stein's moods had been invading my mind, causing me to lose focus on the lesson. Although I couldn't hear what she was thinking, I could sense something wasn't right with my teacher.

Mrs. Stein smiled reassuringly. "You need to find the 'Y'."

"I found it." I pointed to my equation. "It's a letter. It's on the board."

"Duh, Sophie," AJ laughed. "What does it stand for?"

I was beyond frustration. "Why do we need a 'Y'? Why can't we just use a number? Letters are for English class."

Mrs. Stein's smile thinned. "If we used a number, then you'd have the answer and there'd be nothing to solve."

I threw down my dry-erase marker and flung myself into Mrs. Stein's padded chair. She was the only teacher who'd let me get away with that. "I don't see why learning this is going to help me anyway."

"It helps you develop reasoning and logic skills." Mrs. Stein handed me the marker and pointed to the board. "Try again."

I dragged my reluctant feet over to the board. I was tired and my brain hurt. I didn't want to think about algebra anymore. "I don't see any logic in calling letters numbers."

Mrs. Stein took a deep breath and closed her eyes. I could tell she was silently counting to ten. I knew there were days when I tried her patience but I really didn't like algebra. Still, I admired Mrs. Stein for the countless after-school hours she spent tutoring boneheads like me. The fact she never gave up on me was what kept me coming back for more torture.

AJ understood algebra. I didn't know why she hung around, other than to nag me and maybe spend a few more hours each week away from her mother.

I was seven weeks into school and so utterly confused in my algebra class, I felt like I was falling off a cliff in a nightmare, only I couldn't wake up.

"I don't think I'm getting through to you." Mrs. Stein exhaled deeply and sank into her chair. "Maybe you need a peer tutor."

"I can tutor her, Mrs. Stein." AJ tossed her ponytail and smiled.

"No, you two are too close," Mrs. Stein laughed. "No offense, but I don't think you'd get any work done."

She was right. As much time as we spent goofing off in class, I couldn't blame Mrs. Stein for wanting a different tutor. "Who can tutor me, Mrs. Stein? I'm hopeless."

"Just hang on." She patted her book like a baby. "You'll get it."

"No, really, everything was so easy in pre-algebra, but when it comes to algebra, I'm brain dead."

Mrs. Stein jumped up from her chair and shook her finger in my face. "Don't say that. Don't ever say that." Clutching her book to her chest, she rushed out the door.

"Now you've done it." AJ nodded to the door as it slammed shut.

I stared helplessly at AJ. My favorite teacher, my mentor, just threw a tantrum. Was it something I said or did this have to do with whatever was plaguing her mind during class? I was overwhelmed by guilt. Caught up in my own problems, I'd not realized Mrs. Stein's situation was worse than I'd imagined. "What'd I say?"

AJ shrugged her shoulders. "I don't know."

Just as quickly as she exited, Mrs. Stein returned, smiling as usual, still clutching her book. Mrs. Stein was trying hard to mask her feelings but there was something underneath the happy façade. I sensed her dark inner turmoil. Through her frozen smile and glossy eyes, deep into her soul, she hid a hollow, aching pain and it took every scrap of willpower for her to hold back the flood of tears.

She kept smiling, her knuckles turning white from the firm grasp she had on the algebra book. "I'm sorry, Sophie, it just pains me to hear my students speak that way about themselves."

No, that wasn't the problem. She was lying. But what was it? Then I remembered how mad AJ got at me the last time I pried into someone's mind. I wasn't trying to be nosey. I just wanted to help her. I thought about closing my eyes and tuning in Mrs. Stein's inner thoughts, but AJ was beside me and she'd know what I was doing.

I decided to let the issue rest—for now. There would be a better day to fight Mrs. Stein's inner demons. For the present, I decided to focus on fighting my algebra-challenged brain. "Who will you get to tutor me, Mrs. Stein?"

She sat at her desk and faced her computer screen. "He's in Mrs. Hamilton's honors algebra class. He's very gifted."

He...sounded interesting, but *he* couldn't be Jacob. He was in regular algebra, like me. "Who?"

"Frankie Salas."

Frankie Salas, the hottest guy in school? Not him. Anyone but him. I didn't want him to know how stupid I was and not just because he was hot. He could tell Jacob I was a moron. "Isn't there anyone else?"

Mrs. Stein stared at me like I'd just grown an arm out of my head. "What's wrong with Frankie? All the girls like him."

Exactly. I didn't want to be added to his flock of drooling dimwits. "Not *all* the girls."

"How about someone from our class?" Mrs. Stein suggested.

I hesitated, conducting a mental inventory of the possible losers I'd get stuck with if I agreed. I couldn't think of anyone too repulsive. "Okay."

"Cody Miller understands algebra pretty well."

Mrs. Stein pointed to Cody in the far corner of the room. Unaware we were watching, he tutored some of his nerdy friends, while simultaneously picking a wedgie.

How could I have forgotten Grody Cody Miller? He stunk to high heaven. It was rumored Cody only washed his underwear once a week and I believed it. "Maybe Frankie won't be so bad."

"Great." Mrs. Stein tapped her keyboard. "I'll email his math teacher and set it up before school since Frankie has football practice after school."

"Of course."

I knew this all to well, as Lara and I had been to the field twice to take pictures of practice. Both times Jacob sat the bench, completely oblivious to my presence. Frankie had kept looking at us and twice he made me miss a good shot because he'd distracted me with his penetrating eyes. He'd made some impressive plays, but I think he was just showing off for Lara.

Just the thought of the hottest guy in school as my private tutor caused butterflies to form in my stomach. Even though I liked Jacob, not Frankie, something about that boy made girls melt in his presence. How could I survive such a close encounter with Frankie Salas without making a fool of myself?

****

"Isn't Rose Marie in the middle of her semester? Why is she coming home?" I sat with my legs crossed on top of my mom's huge bed and snuggled one of her pillows.

I had gone into her room to get advice. Tomorrow morning, I was supposed to meet with Frankie, and for some reason, my stomach was doing flips. I didn't like

Frankie. I liked Jacob. Everybody liked Frankie. Why would I want to be like everybody else? Besides, Frankie would never be interested in me.

As usual, my problem wasn't important and the topic strayed to one of my perfect sisters.

"She didn't say why she's coming home." My mom chewed nervously on her lip while she paced the floor. "She just said she had something important to tell us."

My sister, Rose Marie, was five years older than me, beautiful and brilliant, everything I wasn't. As the valedictorian of her class and the state debate champ, colleges had lined up at our door for her. Why she chose to go to a public university in Arizona when Dartmouth and Harvard offered her full tuition was beyond me.

My mom suspected Rose Marie's decision had something to do with Chad, Rose Marie's loser boyfriend. The family had hoped she'd dump him after high school. No such luck. He moved to Arizona to work for his uncle's trucking company and Rose Marie had followed.

"I'm so worried about her." A deep line formed in the middle of mom's forehead. She was way tense.

"She'll be fine, Mom. Rose Marie's smart."

"She's good with books, Sophie, not life." Mom pointed to Rose Marie's homecoming picture. "Look at her boyfriend. What did he do with himself after high school?"

I studied the picture. Rose Marie, adorned in her crown and velvet robe, was the model of elegance and beauty. Her escort, on the other hand, was clad in a tuxedo jacket, denim shorts, high-tops with holes in the toes, and a lopsided, unshaven grin. He looked like he lived out of his car. The funny thing was Chad actually was living out of his car when he took that picture. His parents kicked him out of the house after he'd thrown an all night party when they went away for the weekend.

"He didn't do much with himself *in* high school," I quipped.

Mom sighed and put her hand on her hip. "You're not helping."

"Sorry."

Waving her hands in the air, Mom looked like a woman on the edge. "What does she see in him?"

This question has nagged my mother's poor brain

ever since Rose Marie came home her senior year of high school with Chad's rock on her engagement finger. My mom cried, my dad made her take it off, but I saw her wearing it when my parents weren't looking.

"Maybe she's coming home to tell us she broke up with him."

"She could do that over the phone." My mom crossed her arms over her chest and chewed on her thumbnail. "She's missing school. She must have dropped out."

"Now, Mom, don't jump to conclusions." I got off the bed and put my arm around her. "You're getting yourself worked up for no reason. Try to stay calm until she can explain herself."

"If Rose Marie only had your common sense. I never have to worry about you, Sophie."

I hadn't heard my mother say anything like that before. I always thought I had been the dorky disappointment, the problem child. I backed away to get a good look at my mom. "Then why'd you put me in private school?"

"It was a precaution. You've proved us wrong, Sweetie. Look at my baby, growing up into a beautiful, mature young lady." She cupped my chin in her hand and stroked my cheek.

Never had I received such warm praise from my mom. Sure, she gave love in abundance, but she's my mom and I'm the baby. This was the first time Mom saw me as someone other than her fat little munchkin. Or maybe just the first time I knew she did.

I smiled at my mom and savored the moment. Lately, I'd been too busy with my friends or school to spend time with her. Rose Marie had been out of the house for over three months. With my oldest sister, Lu Lu, in med school, I was the only child and I needed to soak up some of Mom's affection more often. I made a mental note to do more things with my mom as soon as Rose Marie went back to college. Hopefully, my sister would only be home for a few days.

Our mother-daughter bonding was cut short by the sound of the doorbell. Mom turned, and without a second glance, raced downstairs.

Dad had already let them in, Rose Marie...and Chad.

He was holding her suitcase; she was holding his hand with her other hand resting on her stomach.

I did a double take. Was Rose Marie, my perfect sister, getting fat?

My dad swore, my mom wailed like a baby.

I thought, "Hey, parents, chill, it's just the freshman fifteen. Lots of students gain weight their first year in college."

Then it hit me.

Chapter Eight

"So now they're living with you?" Eyes wide, AJ leaned over the bus seat, eagerly taking in my family gossip.

I wanted to tell them last night, but by the time my parents were through with their lecture, it was past midnight. I wasn't about to miss my sister getting her butt royally chewed.

"Yeah. I have to give up my bedroom."

"That sucks," AJ complained. "You just moved into that room."

"You shouldn't have to move because they're stupid."

Krysta was right, but I had no choice. When I refused to give up my room, Rose Marie cried, making my mom sob all over again.

"It's closest to the bathroom." I rolled my eyes. "Rose Marie goes at least five times a night."

AJ narrowed her eyes. "What is she going to do about college?"

"She wants to be a stay-at-home mom." I said this with bitterness in my voice. I couldn't help it. The idea of my sister and Chad having a baby was totally absurd.

Krysta laughed. "She doesn't even *have* a home."

"My mother would have sent her packing," AJ said.

"That's what my dad wanted to do, but my mom said we must think about the baby."

"Does Chad still have a job?" AJ's question was the first thing my dad asked Chad last night.

"Yeah, thank God. He works for his uncle's trucking company, so he will be gone three weeks, home one." Getting used to living with my sister again, and a baby would be difficult, but the thought of sharing a bathroom with her new husband made me sick. "I hope he keeps this job. He lost a lot of jobs in high school because of his stupidity."

"I thought your sister was perfect, Sophie," AJ flipped her ponytail and turned up her nose, "but she really screwed up."

"Remember how we all wanted to be like her?" Krysta shook her head in amazement.

"Not anymore." We all said this simultaneously, looked at each other with knowing grins, and laughed. It was scary how my friends and I thought alike.

"Well, Sophie," Krysta sounded optimistic, "this has got to be good for you."

"How can you say that? I lost my room. I won't be the baby anymore."

AJ straightened. "At least you won't have to compete with your perfect sister."

"Lu Lu is the top student in her medical school," I reminded her. Although Lu Lu rarely called because of her hectic school schedule, our living room walls were plastered with certificates of achievement from my brainy oldest sister.

"That can be you someday," AJ pointed out. "You won't come home from college knocked up by some loser."

"No, I won't." I didn't know why, but my mind drew a picture of Jacob at AJ's loser comment—Jacob sitting the bench, Jacob playing video games in English class, Jacob getting sent to the office. But it was unfair of me to compare him to Chad, wasn't it? After all, this was just the ninth grade. A guy can change a lot over four years.

****

He was waiting in Mrs. Stein's classroom—alone. I didn't know why I expected Frankie not to show up, but he was there, casually leaning back in his desk with his hands folded behind his head, smiling.

I slipped my backpack off my shoulder and tried my best to smile back as I sat in a desk facing him. Knowing how close I was to Frankie made my insides quiver. His heady cologne slowly wrapped its coils around my senses. I tried to back away from the temptation, but there was nowhere to go. These desks hadn't been positioned so closely before.

"So." Frankie grabbed a pencil from his binder. "Mrs. Stein said you don't get algebra."

As I stared into those deep, brown eyes, I nodded but

57

said nothing.

He smiled and opened a book. "Let's start with the basics."

"Uh, huh." I couldn't think, didn't know how to act around Frankie Salas. Words trickled from my mouth but I was powerless over what I said. I was behaving like a complete idiot. And over Frankie? I needed to get a grip. I didn't even like the guy.

Frankie picked up his pencil and scribbled something on a piece of paper. "Mrs. Stein told me you get fractions and percentages, but you get stuck on equations."

"Yeah." Why was the sexiest guy in school willing to tutor me? Why was Mrs. Stein nowhere to be found? Was she just going to leave me alone with him?

"Sophie?" Frankie leaned closer.

I was struck with a rush of cool, minty air. Dentyne Ice. The boy was on fire. I jerked up to see Frankie's lopsided grin. He was facing the paper toward me. I looked at his equation.

$S + F = 2$

"Mrs. Stein told me you don't understand why we use letters instead of numbers. So imagine 'S' stands for the initial of a person." Frankie pointed to the equation. "Who do you know whose name begins with an 'S'?"

Somewhere, in the furthest corner of my mind, I suspected the answer he wanted but was too nervous to give it. "Sally?"

"Sally?" He set down the pencil and rubbed his jaw. "I don't know a girl named Sally."

I smiled and bit my lip. "I made her up."

"Alright. Give me the name of someone beginning with an 'F'."

His voice was deep for a guy his age, yet so soft, I had to lean closer to hear him. "Fritz."

He quirked an eyebrow. "Fritz?"

I felt the heat rising in my cheeks. I grabbed the pencil and squeezed, as I tried to still my shaking fingers. "You wanted a name."

"You're right." He flashed a teasing grin. "Let's take Sally and Fritz, for example." Frankie reached for the pencil.

I jumped at the contact of his skin on mine. I could

feel my face redden even before he had time to react.

"I need the pencil." He waved his fingers. "So I can finish the equation."

"I'm sorry." I clenched the pencil and tried to squeeze all the nervousness out of my body. Frankie Salas was flirting with me and I didn't understand why. I was too nervous to read his mind. Because I was so nervous, I couldn't even focus on my own thoughts.

His deep brown eyes found mine. "Is there something wrong?" I felt my body tingle at the feel of his penetrating gaze.

"No. I just don't like algebra."

A good excuse, but not hardly the truth. Something was wrong with me and I was feeling incredibly foolish for my nervousness. I wasn't in love with Frankie. The rest of the female population was. So why did I have to remind myself of this? Frankie was a player and I wasn't about to be added to his list of love-sick admirers.

He wrapped his fingers around mine and gently pried the pencil out of my hand. I felt heat race through my neck, my cheeks and down my spine.

"Now imagine Fritz asks Sophie, sorry, Sally on a date. How many people would that equal on a date?" Frankie winked, not even trying to conceal the mischief brewing in his eyes.

"Two?" I whispered. I couldn't tear my gaze from his face.

"Great. Sally plus Fritz equals two people." Frankie scribbled something on the paper.

I breathed out. "Yes."

"So what number does Sally represent?"

"Stupid," I said it without thinking. This was Frankie's fault. He had my brain all mixed up.

Frankie's eyes widened. "What? Stupid's not a number."

"Sorry, I don't know why I said that." I closed my eyes and pretended to think. I knew the answer but I needed some time to settle my nerves. Unfortunately, Frankie was still there when I opened my eyes, still hot, still tempting me with that playful smile. "One."

"That's right, Sally equals one." Frankie reassuringly squeezed my hand.

I thought about pulling free, but something willed me to squeeze back. I was an idiot.

"So how's the lesson coming?" Mrs. Stein's melodic voice broke the spell.

Thank God.

I quickly pulled my hand away and arched back. Now I saw why so many girls had fallen for Frankie Salas. The boy was magic, pure magic.

****

Frankie's magic worked on me throughout the morning, because I floated through my first and second periods. Not until I reached Mrs. Stein's class, and I sat in the very seat Frankie used, did it hit me. Was Frankie just flirting or did he like me?

Impossible.

He went to Greenwood in the seventh grade. He should have remembered the fat me. I must have been just flirting practice. He was probably warming up for another girl, a cool girl.

That realization was like a punch to my ribcage. But why did I let it bother me? After all, I liked Jacob, not Frankie.

I tried to focus on Mrs. Stein's lesson, but it was difficult with so much on my mind. But, knowing I was going to be even further behind, I forced my mind to go blank.

Why didn't you take me, too? The sound of Mrs. Stein's agonizing plea threw my brain off kilter. I looked into her haunted expression. What was she thinking? Take her where? Who was she speaking to?

Our eyes made contact. I looked away, ashamed for invading her thoughts. She didn't know I knew what she was thinking. Did she?

"Sophie, stay a minute. I want to talk to you."

The entire class oohed and aahed at the seriousness in her voice.

I sank in my seat. She couldn't have known I was invading her thoughts. "Sure, Mrs. Stein."

The bell rang and I watched my classmates file out. Some of them whispered and looked in my direction. Kids were so nosey and annoying. I figured that's how the rest of my peers had to act when they didn't have the power to read minds.

Clutching her book and timidly smiling, Mrs. Stein settled in the desk in front of me. "You never answered my question."

"What question?" Did she ask me to give an answer when I was mentally absent today? When I was reading her mind?

She leaned forward. "How'd the tutoring go?"

"Oh, fine." I sighed in relief. All this worrying about Frankie was turning me into a nervous wreck.

"Oh, really?" Her voice rose several octaves. "You were red as a beet when I walked in. Does he make you feel uncomfortable? I can find a new tutor."

"No!" Somehow, I'd said that way too quickly. Exhaling deeply, I tried to relax my tense shoulders. "What I mean is, that's okay, Mrs. Stein. He was just telling a joke."

"Good." She patted my hand. "You're a smart girl and I want to see you catch up."

Overcome by disbelief, I stared at her. "You think I'm smart?"

"Of course. Why wouldn't I?" Mrs. Stein shrugged her shoulders. "You know your sister struggled in math."

"My sister? Which one?" Impossible. They were both Valedictorians.

"Rose Marie."

My jaw dropped. Up until the marriage and pregnancy, Rose Marie led a flawless life, too smart to be stupid in math. "I think you have her mixed up with someone else. Rose Marie was Valedictorian."

Mrs. Stein sighed and shook her head. "I didn't say she *failed* math. She struggled, but she went to tutoring every day and caught up."

Could my math brain finally grow, too? "You think that could happen to me?"

"You have to believe in yourself, Sophie."

She was beginning to sound like AJ and Krysta. But she was right.

I shrugged. "That's something I'm working on."

"Keep working on it, dear. You've got a lot going for you. Remember, don't let anything or *anyone* make you think any different." Mrs. Stein looked at me from under her eyelids.

For a minute, I thought *she* was reading *my* mind. Could she have heard about the way Jacob expected me to cheat for him or how Summer bullied me? "Thanks, Mrs. Stein."

"Anytime." She stood up and propped open the door. "If you ever need to talk, my room is open."

"Okay, I'll remember." I didn't need to talk; what I needed was to act, starting with the bully who plagued my passing periods.

****

I had my eyes on my target. I was ready, charged to take command. Summer spoke to her best friend, Marisela, while leaning against my locker door. I knew she wasn't going to move unless I made her.

This was it. I was either going to get my butt royally kicked or I would finally get some respect. No turning back.

"I think Frankie Salas is going to ask me to the Freshmen Formal dance." Summer sighed and ran her fingers through her hair.

I froze. What was wrong with me? Even the mention of his name made my heart skip. I hunched over, pretending to be fumbling something out of my backpack while I listened to their conversation.

"How do you know?" Marisela looked in Summer's mirror while layering on tons of bright red lipstick.

"The boy can't keep his eyes off me. He's so pathetic." Summer laughed and looked straight at me.

Her eyes danced in mock delight which made me want to punch her.

Of all the girls Frankie could have picked at this school, why Summer? Why couldn't he see she was a self-centered and fake, not to mention stupid? Summer flirted with every guy in school just to get attention.

"Are you going to go with him?" Marisela closed Summer's locker door and slipped her leather Dooney and Bourke purse over her shoulder.

"I don't know. There's a Britney Spears concert on VH-1 that weekend." She shrugged, examining her fake fingernails. "I'll have to think about it."

They both sauntered off with heads held high, two

cosmetic cretins, laughing and saying hello to every guy within twenty yards.

I was stunned, mortified. I shouldn't have cared one bit. I didn't like Frankie. I liked Jacob. I had to remind myself several times throughout the morning, I liked Jacob. His puppy dog eyes, his small ears and masculine thighs. So, why couldn't I get Frankie Salas out of my mind?

****

I silently walked into the yearbook room and sunk into my chair.

Lara sat beside me and put a hand on my shoulder. "What's wrong?"

I sighed and listlessly tapped my computer mouse. "Frankie Salas is going to ask Summer Powers to the Freshmen Formal dance."

"Yuk," Lara frowned. "He could pick any girl in this school."

"Yeah, I know."

Last Friday at a football game, Lara had finally told me that last year Summer had started the slut rumors. I knew why. Summer was jealous. Lara had this crazy idea Summer was jealous of me, too.

"Why do you care?" She paused, and then frowned. "You like Jacob, right?"

"Yeah," I hesitated, "I like Jacob." I felt a wave of guilt wash over me. Although she never confessed Jacob was the guy on the bus who called her a slut, I noticed she always seemed reluctant to bring up his name.

She flashed me a mischievous smile and leaned closer. "Can you keep a secret?"

I hesitated. If this was about Jacob, she wouldn't be smiling. "Sure, you can tell me anything, Lara."

Lara opened PhotoShop on her computer and went into a folder marked "Lara's Secrets". I had never seen that folder on the network. She must have had it hidden on her computer.

Lara clicked on a file marked 'Dallin's Twin'. The picture that popped up nearly knocked me out of my seat. Summer with her finger shoved up her nose had to be some sort of trick, some awesome, hilarious trick.

My mouth fell open. "How did you get that?"

"I was behind a bathroom stall with my zoom lens," Lara whispered. "She didn't even see me."

I couldn't believe I was actually looking at a picture of Summer Powers picking her nose. This was no ordinary pick. This was a good, solid half-an-inch pick. A pick that could rival Dallin's digging any day.

"What are you going to do with this?" I asked.

"Mrs. Carr would kill me if I used this in the yearbook. I'm saving it for just the right time." She grinned and rubbed her hands together.

"Any idea when that special moment might be?"

I couldn't wait to see Summer exposed. When Lara unveiled her masterpiece, I wanted a front row seat.

"No, but when the timing's right." She laughed. "I'm using it."

****

"Earth to Sophie." AJ stared from over the top of the puke-green, fake leather bench in front of me. "What are you smiling about?"

I couldn't help daydreaming on the bus ride home. I imagined Summer crying and gobs of mascara running down her face as the entire student body laughed and pointed at a life sized poster of her big dig hanging in the school auditorium.

I let a small chuckle escape. "I was just thinking of something funny that happened today."

Krysta slouched next to me with her knees resting on the back of AJ's seat. She peered from over her *Cosmo*. "Are you going to clue us in?"

"Sorry." I shook my head. "I promised to keep it secret."

"Aaahhh, you suck!" AJ punched the top of her cushioned seat.

AJ and Krysta both sighed and eyed me intently.

I raised my palms and shrugged. "Sorry, guys."

They pleaded with their best Patches' puppy dog impressions, but I wasn't about to give in.

Luckily, the bus driver distracted them. He took a sharp right and we almost slid onto the floor.

Krysta's *Cosmo* flew out of her grasp and landed across the aisle in Cody Miller's lap. He smiled and handed her the magazine. Krysta shuddered as she retrieved her *Cosmo* with the tips of her fingers and then she shook it a few times as we watched imaginary germs fall to the floor.

She put *Cosmo* in her backpack and scooted closer to me. "How's living with your sister and her new husband working out?"

Thank God Krysta changed the subject. My promise to keep Lara's secret was important. I needed Lara to know she could trust me with anything. "It's not. Chad quit his job working for his uncle. Imagine that." I rolled my eyes. "He says he can't be a daddy and be gone all the time."

"He can't be a daddy if he doesn't pay the bills, either." Krysta always made perfect sense.

"I don't think he gets it yet," I complained. "Anyway, he says he wants a job here, but I don't see him looking for one. All he does is eat everything in sight and leave messes all over the house."

"Do you pick up after him?" AJ asked.

I glared at AJ. "What do you think? He left his rotten underwear on my bathroom floor this morning. I stepped on them with my bare feet."

"Eeeewww." AJ and Krysta said in unison as they shrunk back in disgust.

I crinkled my nose. "I banged on their door and Rose Marie picked them up. You should see how she babies him." I used to be jealous of Rose Marie, but now it made me sick to see that my perfect sister had sunk so low. She could have been studying medicine at Harvard, but instead she was playing janitor to her dung pile husband.

"Puke." AJ stuck her finger in her mouth and made the universal sign of vomit.

"Yeah," I laughed. "My dad said she won't have time to baby him when the real baby comes."

Krysta's brow drew a frown. "I'm surprised your dad hasn't kicked them out yet."

I had been dreaming of seeing their backsides ever since they showed up at our door. "My mom won't let him," I sighed. "She's starting to really get on my nerves, too."

Krysta's eyes widened. "Why?"

"Ever since Rose Marie came home, it's been Rose

Marie this or baby that. You should see the money my mom has spent. She already bought a crib and they're painting dinosaurs all over *my* bedroom. They didn't even ask me."

"I don't think it's *your* bedroom anymore, Sophie," Krysta reminded me.

AJ leaned forward and narrowed her gaze. "You sound jealous, Sophie."

"Jealous?" I snapped, ready to tear off AJ's head. "How could you say that, AJ? Why would you think I'm jealous? They've just thrown their lives down the toilet and you think I'm jealous?"

AJ leaned back and shrugged. "You don't have to get so defensive. It was just an observation."

"I'm not jealous." The pitch in my voice rose. "It just pisses me off that Rose Marie screws up and she gets the royal treatment. Mom wouldn't do that for me."

"Yep." AJ waved her finger at me. "That's jealousy."

"You know, AJ," I folded my arms across my chest. "I'm really getting sick of your negative comments." I had enough to deal with at home, being pushed aside by my family, forced to give up my room, because Rose Marie screwed up her life. I didn't need crap from my best friend, too.

"What?" Her mouth gaped. AJ actually had the nerve to act surprised.

"A friend comes to you with her problems and all you do is bring her down."

AJ had been on a negative trip lately and I was tired of her PMS.

"Look." AJ waved her head, pretending she was tough. "Don't get all pissy because your family life sucks. Welcome to my world. I deal with this kind of crap all the time."

"Okay, enough." Krysta put out both hands and glared at me before throwing visual daggers at AJ. "This is getting us nowhere." She looked out the window as the bus slowed. "This is your stop. Now you two kiss and make up."

We both rolled our eyes and stubbornly crossed our arms over our chests.

"Remember, we're all best friends." Krysta smiled

and punched me playfully on the shoulder. "Sophie, try not to kill your new brother."

I felt like slapping her for that comment, but I stuck out my tongue instead. She had a way of always finding humor in even the worst situations.

Chapter Nine

How was I going to finish my homework with that
noise in the next room? I banged on the wall, my third
attempt to get Chad to turn down the volume on his video
game. I couldn't believe this moron was about to be a dad.

As expected, Chad didn't respond.

I stormed downstairs just as my mom and Rose
Marie came through the door. Rose Marie had her arm
around Mom's shoulder when they walked into the living
room with tons of baby store bags, compliments of my
parents' bank account no doubt.

I couldn't deny it. I was annoyed and I had a right to
be. Rose Marie was kissing up to Mom, so she and that
bum upstairs could keep getting free rent.

Rose Marie whispered something into Mom's ear and
they both started laughing.

This nonsense had to stop.

"Would someone tell that jerk upstairs to turn down
his video game?"

Rose Marie's smile diminished, replaced by a cold
glare. "What's your problem?"

"Some of us have homework to do, Rose Marie. Some
of us want to make something of ourselves." An
unnecessary jab, but I was beyond irritated.

"What in the hell is that supposed to mean?" Rose
Marie threw back her shoulders and stormed up to me.

"Girls, no fighting, please." Mom got in between us
and turned to me. "Sophie, you shouldn't speak to Rose
Marie in her condition."

"I didn't know *stupid* was a condition."

"That's enough, young lady." Mom's voice hardened.
"Show some respect."

"I'll show respect when *he* does." I pointed toward the
stairs. "I've been trying to get him to turn down his game
for over an hour. How did he afford a video game,

anyway? I thought he lost his job."

Rose Marie crossed her arms over her chest. "How we spend our money is none of your business."

"What money?" I snapped. "You don't have any."

"Chad just got his last paycheck." Rose Marie tried to look me in the eyes, but she quickly averted her gaze.

I could tell defending Chad was difficult, even for someone as blind as my sister.

I laughed. "So he buys a Play Station?"

"For your information, the Play Station is for the baby, too." Her shaky voice lowered, sounding less convincing. "It plays DVDs, you know."

"Of course." I threw my hands in the air. "A Play Station will be first on my list when I have a baby. Maybe he should save up for the baby, or here's a concept, maybe he should be out looking for another job."

"He has his applications in." Rose Marie looked at the floor. "He's just waiting for call backs."

"Yeah, right." How did Rose Marie expect me to buy this crap when she didn't even look convinced? Chad didn't want a job—he liked being a bum. He was using this baby as an excuse to stay home and play video games.

"Sophie," my mom pleaded. "They've already heard this from your father. This isn't your concern."

"Not my concern?" I couldn't contain the bitterness in my voice. "I gave up *my* room. *She* wakes me up all night with her bladder. I can't even do my homework in peace! And this is none of *my* concern!"

Mom faced my sister and gently stroked her cheek. "Rose Marie, sweetie, go upstairs and tell Chad to turn it down." Mom turned to me, her frown full of disappointment.

I hated letting my mom down more than anything, which only aggravated me more. This was all Rose Marie's fault. "Yeah, why don't you do that?" I yelled to my retreating sister. "That will just solve everything. While you're at it, why don't you tell him to go find another job?"

"You sound just like Dad." My sister yelled at me as she climbed the stairs. "I don't need to be nagged by two of you."

I ran to the foot of the stairwell and shouted. "I can't

believe two immature idiots are bringing a baby into this world."

Rose Marie quickly backtracked down the steps and raised her open palm. "If Mom wasn't here, I'd slap you."

"Go ahead," I warned. "I'd slap back if I knew it was a cure for stupid. When are you going to wake up? He's a bum, a loser. You and the baby will always have to borrow from Mom and Dad."

Rose Marie's angry expression froze, her widening eyes showed amusement as she revealed a broad smile. "Sounds to me like you're jealous."

"Yeah, right." I looked away. I was annoyed, not jealous. I did *not* want her to misinterpret one for the other.

"You won't be the baby anymore," she mocked. "You're not going to get all the attention."

"Girls, you're giving me a headache. Enough!" Mom placed both hands on her forehead.

I was just getting warmed up. I had a lot more to say to Rose Marie. If it hadn't been for the tears I could see forming in my mom's eyes, I wouldn't have backed down.

My sister turned on her heel and ran into *my* bedroom. I stormed up to my new room and slammed the door while contemplating revenge against the idiots who were ruining my life and driving a wedge between my mom and me. I needed to get my frustration off my chest. I opened my cell and dialed Krysta.

The call went straight to her voice mail. My only other option was AJ. Even though I was mad at her, I had to vent to someone.

I dialed her number.

"What's up?" AJ sounded annoyed. I knew she knew it was me calling because all of the phones in her house had Caller ID.

"Hey," I blurted. "Chad's a butt munch."

"So tell me something I don't know," AJ retorted.

I was so furious, complaints started spewing from my mouth. "He hasn't even bothered to look for a job. He played video games all day while my mom spent money on his baby."

"Pathetic."

AJ's reaction wasn't what I expected. She almost

sounded bored. Probably just my imagination.

"Yeah," I sighed in frustration. "What a bum."

"Sounds like another guy I know." AJ's tone was definitely on the rude side.

"Let me guess," I said sarcastically. I knew where she was going with this. "You're talking about Jacob."

"You're as blind as your sister when it comes to guys." AJ paused before groaning. "Just think, this could be you and Jacob in four years."

"That's not funny."

"I'm not trying to be funny," AJ snapped. "Your sister doesn't have taste in guys and neither do you. You're both too stupid to admit it."

"I gotta go." Her PMS had pushed my temper past the limit.

"Fine," She fumed. "Don't listen to a friend."

I yelled into the phone. "Friends don't call each other stupid."

"Whatever." AJ's defensive, sarcastic tone was the same way she spoke to her mother. "Throw your life away then."

"I'm not throwing my life away." I could feel my throat tighten as I tried to hold back tears. "I haven't even gotten Jacob to notice me."

"I don't understand." AJ growled, set down the phone, swore loudly and then picked the receiver up again. "You want to be cool so Jacob will like you, Sophie. Cheating for him isn't cool. Try not letting him walk all over you, that's cool."

"Look, I gotta go." An aggravated laugh escaped my lips. "Thanks for cheering me up." I slammed the phone, hoping it would make me feel better. It didn't.

How could she say such things about Jacob? Just because he liked video games, just because he wasn't great at sports and didn't like to read, didn't mean he'd end up like Chad. Besides, he *had* to be the one. He was fat once, just like me. He was the only guy who'd understand me. Not like Frankie. That boy was born perfect. He'd never take a former fatty seriously. Even if he really did like me, one day he'd wake up and remember the former me. He'd find my seventh grade yearbook picture and he'd move on to a new groupie.

I fell onto my bed and closed my eyes. Maybe after our novel unit was over, Jacob would pay more attention in class. Maybe if I could prove to him I was cool, he might even forget his video game and pay more attention to me. Because that's what I wanted, right? A nagging little voice in the back of my conscience whispered AJ was right, but I didn't want to listen. I was destined for Jacob, because...well, I just wasn't good enough for Frankie.

Chapter Ten

The Scarlet letter, would the torture ever end? I thought Huck Finn was bad. The only amusing part in reading this new novel was when Cody Miller taped a big fat crimson "B" on Dallin's back.

Dallin didn't even notice. He was too busy picking his nose.

We had finished Huck a few weeks ago and now we were starting chapter four of this interminable book. We'd had a couple of pop quizzes but so far Jacob still hadn't graded a single one of my tests. We'd passed them to the left, to the right, and backward, but never forward. Jacob had lucked out two more times since I'd first graded his test. I didn't like cheating for him, but I had no choice if I was to follow through with my plan.

The ironic thing was this whole plan to see if Jacob cared for me was starting not to matter. I had intentionally missed several questions on the last three tests. After I'd brought home a C on my progress report, I decided enough was enough.

Although I was hesitant to admit it, the disappointed look on my parents' faces wasn't the only reason I chose to ace all future tests. Frankie had graded my tests twice. He must have thought I was stupid at math and in English. Not that his opinion mattered that much.

I had just finished answering the last question on my quiz when Dallin told us to pass our tests to the back.

Jacob handed me his test and his pen, giving me a sly wink. He didn't even say anything. It was like he expected, no demanded, and 'A' from me now. Suddenly, his cute ears weren't so cute anymore. They were too small and starting to annoy me.

I reluctantly took his test and his pen.

I remembered AJ's harsh words from the argument we had on the phone. "Cheating for him isn't cool. Try not letting him walk all over you, that's cool."

I had been thinking about those words all day—while I was ignoring her on the bus ride to school, while she was ignoring me in algebra, while we both ignored each other at lunch. I thought of little else. AJ could be a real pain in the butt sometimes, but she was my best friend. Was I wrong to completely ignore her advice?

Mr. Dallin perched himself on top of a wobbly stool, ready to call out answers.

Without a second to spare, I reacted quickly. "Here, I don't need this." I handed Jacob his pen and took out my own pink pen—bright enough to emphasize any glaring mistakes.

Jacob's eyes widened, and then narrowed, as he snatched his pen from my hand.

I smiled back while keeping my cool. I could hear Frankie's muffled laughter beside me.

By the time grading was over, Jacob had a D minus and I had some of my self-respect back. Jacob was pissed, but to quote Frankie, "He'll get over it."

I left a little note on his test, too. "Jacob, put away the video game and study harder." I thought I saw steam shooting out of his puny ears when he was reading it.

****

"I hope this game doesn't run into overtime." Lara leaned her chin on the body of her camera, while her knee settled against her monopod. She looked the part of a professional photographer. She even wore a photo vest.

"Why?" I wondered. "It's just getting fun."

We were in the middle of the fourth quarter. Frankie had just scored a touchdown and the crowd was pumped. I got lots of great shots of screaming fans. Lara caught Frankie just as he made the touchdown. I would get Lara to save me a copy of that picture later.

"Yeah," she looked up and frowned. "But we're losing the good light and this camera doesn't take the best night shots." Lara reached into her bag and retrieved some ancient relic that looked like a camera. "My K-1000 won't fail me."

"How do you use it?"

She smiled. "It runs on this weird fuel called film." She grabbed a roll of film out of her bag and started to manually wind the film into the camera. It looked complicated.

"I'll stick with the digital camera." I patted my Digital Rebel, my baby, actually Mrs. Carr's baby. She practically made me sign in blood that I would protect it with my life.

"Stay here while I go to the fifty yard line." Lara gathered up her gear and started to walk away.

"But what if someone makes a touchdown?" I felt uneasy by myself. I was still new at this.

"Then take the shot," she called back.

"What if I mess up?" I squeezed the leather straps on my camera, trying to calm my fears. Lara had never left me alone to take pictures. What if something bad happened?

Lara walked toward me and put her hand on my shoulder. "There will be plenty more touchdowns. You have no confidence in yourself, Sophie. Your pictures have been coming out great. You're a natural."

I hadn't received a compliment like that in a long time. My chest swelled up with pride. "Really? A natural?"

"I don't lie." As Lara headed back to the fifty-yard-line, she called over her shoulder. "Not when it comes to photography. Remember, follow the ball, not the players, if you want the best shot. Believe me, wherever that ball goes, they'll go too."

"Gotcha," I yelled.

I looked through the LCD, poised, focused, ready. I was going to get that picture of Frankie Salas, or whoever, making the touchdown. It was going to be so awesome; Mrs. Carr would want to put it on the cover of the yearbook.

I heard someone yell, "Look out," but I was in the photo zone, too focused to pay attention to anything else but that pigskin.

Hey, where'd it go? I had the ball in focus just a minute ago.

Thunk.

****

"Sophie, you okay?"

Was this a dream? I opened my eyes to the sight of Frankie standing over me. Although my vision was a bit fuzzy, I could still make out his beautiful tanned skin and

I couldn't mistake his deep voice. I tried to sit up, when I was suddenly struck by a dizzying sensation. The room shook and I fell back against soft padding.

"W...what happened?" The entire left side of my face felt like it had been run over by a steamroller.

"Don't try to get up." Frankie sat by my side and put an icepack on my left eye. "You got hit by the ball."

Did I? I didn't remember. I recalled looking for the ball through my view finder. Oh, God. The camera! Mrs. Carr would have my head on a platter. "Is the camera okay?"

Frankie laughed. "Yeah, it's okay."

"I've got it, Sophie." I heard Lara in the background, but I couldn't see her.

"Where am I?" I touched a hand to my sore cheek and breathed deeply. Wherever I was, the place reeked of musty body odor.

"Lying on a cot at the fieldhouse." Frankie grabbed my hand and placed it over the icepack.

As dizzy as I was, I still felt the electrifying shock of his skin against mine. "Who won?"

"We're in a time-out." He slowly withdrew his hand.

I immediately missed his touch. "I...it's not because of me, is it?"

"Yep." Frankie smiled sympathetically.

I wanted to crawl inside a hole and not come out for at least fifty years. "I feel so stupid. How long have I been out?"

"Only about ten minutes." A masculine voice came from the other side of my cot.

I tried to turn my head to make out his figure, but my neck was too stiff.

"Is she going to be okay, Schotts?" Frankie asked.

I recognized that name. Schotts was the team medic. Now I felt really dumb. He should have been with the team, not me.

"Yeah," Schotts said. "Her mom still needs to get her an x-ray."

Frankie looked down at me, and even through my blurry vision, I could see pity pooling in his huge brown eyes. "Guess that means you'll miss the rest of the game."

My heart felt like it was sinking into a hole, covered

by the sludge of humiliation and self-loathing. I didn't want Frankie's pity. Why did this have to happen to me?

The deep sound of a masculine voice clearing his throat reminded me Frankie wasn't the only person in the room sharing in my shame.

"Listen, I have to get back. Robbins twisted his ankle before Sophie was knocked out." Schotts squeezed my shoulder. "You mom's coming to pick you up." He walked toward the door and nodded to the corner of the room. "Are you staying with her until her mom comes?"

"Of course." I heard Lara's clipped voice as she crossed over to my cot.

"Come on, Frankie. You need to get back in the game," Schotts said.

Frankie stood. "See ya later, Sophie."

"Thanks, Frankie." I called, as his blurred figure moved out of vision.

"No problem." His voice was still near.

"Frankie?" My dizziness was fading, so I sat up halfway, trying to catch him before he left.

"Yeah?"

Through my one good eye, I could see his dark form standing by the open door. "Good luck tonight." I tried to smile, but my face hurt too much.

He looked at his feet, and then turned his gaze outside. "Thanks."

I sighed as I heard the door shut. Frankie couldn't even look at me. What did he think of me? Probably what everybody else thought. I was never going to live this one down. I would have rather been labeled the fat dork than the village idiot.

"Lara," I sank into the cot. "I feel like such a loser."

She sighed. "I think the whole thing is romantic."

"What are you talking about?" I turned on my side to face her. The girl was crazy.

"Frankie has the hots for you. He was the first one to get to you when you were hit."

The giddy sensation in my head was returning, but I didn't think it was because of the hit. "You're lying."

"No, I'm not," she nudged my ribs. "He carried you here."

I felt chills rush through my body. Frankie carried

me! Why would he want to do that? "Okay, now you're really full of it."

"Think what you want," she shrugged, "but I'm sure you'll hear it around school on Monday."

"Oh, God, I'm going to be the laughing stock of Greenwood. I feel like crap and I bet I look like crap, too."

Lara looked at me and cringed. Her expression confirmed my worst fears.

She carefully removed my icepack. "It's mostly your eye."

"Get me a mirror."

Lara squeezed my hand. "I don't think you want me to do that."

I squeezed back. "Please. I need to know if I look as stupid as I feel."

Lara grabbed a compact out of her purse. She cringed as she slowly handed me the mirror.

The reflection took me by complete surprise.

My right side looked perfectly normal. The left side of my face looked like a reddened, five hundred pound troll.

Lara drew back, biting her lip.

"Not bad," I said.

She slowly exhaled. "I'm glad you're taking this well."

"Of course." I tried to smile, although the action hurt my eye which felt like it was caving in on itself. "All I need to do is find another giant pink ogre who thinks this face isn't ugly."

Lara threw back her head and laughed. "I'm sorry, Sophie. I know this isn't funny but I'm glad you can still make jokes."

"At least now Jacob might notice me."

That comment didn't seem to sit well with Lara. She glared and then shook her head. "You shouldn't worry what someone like Jacob Flushman thinks of you."

I leaned on my elbows and sharpened my gaze. "What do you know about him I don't know?"

Lara put down her head and turned from me. "Listen, there's something you should know about Jacob."

"Can you help me? I'm looking for Sophie, Sophie Sinora."

I recognized the sound of my mom's panicked voice.

"I'm here, Mom." I called, and instantly regretted the

sound of my own voice as it echoed in my throbbing skull.

"Oh, thank goodness. Are you okay, sweetie?" Mom rushed up to me, then jumped back when she looked at my face. "Oh, my baby!"

"Try to calm down, dear. She'll be okay." My dad stood behind my mom, placing his hands on her shoulders. He shook his head and winked at me.

I understood Dad's message. Mom panicked easily whenever my sisters or I got hurt. Trying to ignore the pain in my face, I put up a front to calm my mom. "It's not as bad as it looks, Mom."

Mom's jaw twitched and she placed her hands on her hips. "We're going to the hospital."

"See you later, Sophie. I've got your camera." Lara waved as she walked out the door.

I hardly noticed she was leaving. Lara and I left some unspoken words. I feared what she was trying to tell me and was somewhat relieved my parents showed up. Was I being selfish not to want to hear it? Lara had proven to be a good friend and mentor. If it weren't for her, I wouldn't have found an interest in photography. With the exception of the one incident tonight, I thought I had actually found something I was good at. Lara taught me how to make yearbook pages, develop pictures, and she listened to me complain about Summer.

What had Jacob ever done for me?

Chapter Eleven

Humiliation was exhausting. I had hoped my parents would drive me home, so I could crawl under my covers and die. Instead, they took me to the emergency room. My dad stayed at the hospital only long enough to convince my mom I wasn't going to fall down with uncontrollable seizures and foam at the mouth. He had a business trip the next morning, so I didn't mind when he called Chad for a ride. My mom and I waited five hours for the doctor to tell us I had a black eye and a bump on my head.

As we walked to the car, I opened my cell phone to check the time. One fifteen a.m. and three missed messages from AJ. I remembered I had turned off the ringer so I wouldn't be distracted during the game. A whole lot of good that did.

The first two messages were just hang-ups, but on the third message, AJ sounded like she was clearing her throat. After a long pause, she finally spoke. "Hey, it's AJ. Look, I'm sorry I've been such a butthead lately. I've been having a really bad time with my mother and I'm taking it out on everyone else.

"I know you like Jacob. I know you think I hate him, but the truth is I don't want to see you getting hurt. He's not the one for you, Sophie. You don't need to be gifted to see his future is going nowhere. And I think you know it, too."

I could hear AJ take a deep breath before continuing. "There's something else, too. Something I haven't told anyone...I'm not mad at you because you're learning how to control your gift. The truth is I'm getting better at it, too. It scares me, Sophie. I don't want us to get better. I might not want to know what's going to happen next. What if it's bad? What if I'm going to die tomorrow? Or someone I care about?"

"Anyway, call me back when you get this message.

I'll be in my room. I'm grounded this weekend, or at least until tomorrow."

My shoulders slumped against the car door as I thought about AJ's confession. I was not alone. Her gift was increasing, too. What if Krysta's powers were growing stronger? More ghostly visits? I shivered at the thought. At least my life wasn't that bad.

Well, not until Monday anyway, when I'd have to face the entire student body of Greenwood Junior High. Everyone would have heard about the football incident. Even if I wanted to deny it, I couldn't, not with this messed-up face. I tried not to think about the humiliation I'd suffer. My head hurt enough.

What if Frankie thought I was a dork?

"Are you going to get in?"

My mom's voice interrupted my rambling thoughts. She was already inside the car, revving the engine.

I climbed inside and lowered my seat. The pain in my head was throbbing, and the medication the doctor gave me made me sleepy. I wanted to rest my eyes on the way home.

"You're not going to sleep in the car, are you? I'm not dragging you out when we get home." Mom turned on the A/C full blast.

She knew I hated a freezing fan blowing in my face. Reluctantly, I positioned my seat back up, put on my seatbelt, and switched the A/C to low.

"Good." Mom focused on the road and clutched the steering wheel so hard her knuckles turned white. "I want to talk to you anyway."

Sensing a lecture coming on, I rubbed my throbbing temples.

"I know things have been rough this week with your sister and all the drama." Mom emphasized 'drama' and rolled her head.

Was she trying to make me feel like an idiot for fighting with Rose Marie? Afraid to get into an argument with my mom, I said nothing. It was late, I was tired, and my face hurt.

Mom inhaled deeply, and then slowly breathed out. "I just wanted to say…I'm sorry."

Huh? Why was she sorry? She didn't tell Rose Marie

to get married and have a baby. My parents were great role models. They taught all of us responsibility. She couldn't help it my sister was stupid and selfish.

"What I mean to say is I'm sorry this has to hit you right now. I know you're right about Chad. I don't think I've ever told you this, but I was married to someone else when I met your dad."

My jaw dropped. Not *my* mom. She was perfect.

"No, no, it's not what you think," she continued. "We were already separated and I had filed for a divorce." Mom moaned and shook her head. "That was the biggest mistake of my life. His name was Brian. We were married for six months. I didn't listen to my friends when they told me he wasn't the right man. In fact, I lost my best friend over him."

She paused, sounding choked up. Was my mom crying? Mom turned her head, looking out the side window. "Anyway," Mom turned back, the visible lines around her heavy, saddened eyes revealing her pain. "What I'm trying to say is I understand why you are so against Chad. Truth is I can't stand the boy either, however, the more we fight Rose Marie, the more she'll think she has to defend him. I know it sounds stupid, but love is blind sometimes."

No, I didn't think it sounded stupid. I was beginning to understand exactly how blind love was.

Mom tapped on the steering wheel and clenched her jaw. "I know you want the best for your sister. I do, too. It breaks my heart to see her throw her life away over him...and now their poor baby." Mom's voice cracked as a tear slid down her cheek. "But I need you to do something for me, Sophie, and for your sister, too. She'll come around. I know she will. I *hope* she will. You just need to let her make this mistake, and when she's tired of him, we can be there to support her. She won't resent you if you leave the decision to her. If we force them apart, I'm afraid she'll never get the chance to learn on her own."

I thought about what Mom had just said and I knew exactly where she was coming from. Even scarier, I knew exactly where Rose Marie was coming from. I had been judging Rose Marie for making the same mistake I was making. I wondered if my sister had lost any friends over

Chad. Well, I wasn't about to let some slouch with fat thighs get in between me and my friends.

"Mom," I asked, "whatever happened to your best friend?"

"I don't know," she sighed. "We lost touch."

How sad. I couldn't imagine a lifetime without AJ and Krysta.

"Didn't you try to find her after your divorce?"

"No," she smiled bitterly. "I guess there was too much resentment there."

I just couldn't understand it. How could Mom have thrown away her friendship over a guy? "But she was your best friend."

"I know," her voice cracked again, "but things change."

Well, I wasn't about to let things change with my friends. I wanted to call back AJ immediately, but her mom would have been furious if I woke the family and I couldn't IM her because AJ didn't have a computer in her room. What I had to say had to wait until the morning. I silently prayed I'd never lose AJ's friendship.

****

I woke to the sound of Barney the Dinosaur, the latest ringtone download AJ had snuck on my phone. AJ's mom needed to buy her a phone, so she'd leave mine alone. I flipped open the phone—9:30 a.m., incoming call from AJ.

As soon as I hit 'talk', AJ started rambling.

"Hey. I wanted to call you earlier. I waited as long as I could. I heard about what happened last night." She inhaled quickly. "You okay?"

"Oh, God," I moaned and gently explored the swelling on my sore face, "I'm sure the whole world knows by now."

"Yeah," she said softly.

I shook my head and laughed. "You should have told me this was going to happen."

"Very funny." AJ sighed.

I knew what she was thinking. I didn't even have to read her mind. She felt awkward about the message she left on my phone last night. Emotions were difficult for AJ, which made last night's message so special. It took a lot of guts for her to confess her fears, and even more courage for her to apologize.

I sensed she was waiting for me to start. "I got your message."

"Oh, it was nothing," She murmured quickly.

But I knew better. "Thanks."

"No problem."

An awkward silence followed. I knew it was my turn to apologize. "AJ?"

"Yeah?"

"Sorry I've been an idiot." I rubbed my brow, trying to think of the right words. "He's the wrong guy for me. I knew it all along."

"It's okay. We all make mistakes."

I fell back on my pillow and stared at the ceiling. "I don't want to pay for it like my sister."

"Good," she huffed, "I don't want to see you end up like her."

"Believe me." I shuddered at the thought. "I won't." The only way to ensure I didn't end up like Rose Marie was to stay away from losers. I decided it was time to completely erase Jacob from my memory. The first step would be to change the subject. AJ's powers were increasing and I was dying to know if I'd be a dateless dork forever. "So how good are you at it?"

"Getting better every day."

I hesitated, wondering if I was ready for the answer. "Am I going to find the right guy?"

"You'll find lots of right guys, Sophie." AJ sighed as she spoke. "That's not my gift talking. Don't you think it's too soon for you to find *the one*?"

"Yeah, you're right again. Maybe I should just focus on the near future." I closed my eyes. Frankie Salas' penetrating eyes were the first thing to pop into my mind. After the football incident, he would never ask me out.

"That's a good idea."

I sensed some hope in AJ's voice.

What good could happen after last night? I still had a small flicker of hope. "So I wonder if someone will ask me to Freshmen Formal."

"Frankie Salas."

My eyes shot open. Had I just heard her correctly? She must have been joking. "You're full of it."

"Okay," her pitch rose, "whatever."

I couldn't believe what I was hearing. Frankie Salas and me? Impossible. "Did you *see* this or are you guessing?"

"I *saw* it."

The pain in my face was worsening. I closed my eyes and tried not to focus on the throbbing pressure. "If you're lying, I'm going to kick your butt." All this time he'd been flirting with me, could he have *really* liked me?

"I'm not lying." AJ sounded serious.

"Humph." I wasn't convinced.

"What?" She laughed. "I thought you would be happy. He's the hottest guy in school."

Exactly. So why would he want to ask me out? I shook my head in disbelief. Frankie had to have a reason. Then I remembered, he was supposed to ask Summer to the dance. "I heard Summer saying he was going to ask her."

"Eeewww," AJ shrieked into the phone. "Are you sure?"

"I heard her talking about it. She said she'd probably turn him down for a Britney concert."

"Summer talks a lot of smack."

"Maybe, but hottie or not, do I want to go out with Summer's reject?" I couldn't believe this was me talking. Frankie was no reject, but I knew Summer would rub my face in it if I dated him after she turned him down.

"You'd be stupid not to."

I wanted to change the subject. All this talk about Summer and Frankie made my head hurt worse. "What else have you seen?"

"You really want to know?"

"Yeah." I lied. In some ways, I *really* wanted to know. In other ways, AJ's gift scared me to my toes. I doubted my future held anything as bad as the football incident.

"No bad stuff yet, thank God. But," she squealed, "I did see you with your new nephews."

"Nephews?" This was bad news. *Really* bad news. "You mean my stupid sister is going to breed with that worthless dungheap again?"

"No. I mean she's having twins."

"Holy crap!" I thought my life was bad. I would have

picked a black eye over twins any day.

"Yeah. Your sister's gonna be hatin' life." AJ wasn't kidding.

"How long is Chad in her future?" I couldn't imagine him hanging around with two babies to take care of and I couldn't imagine Rose Marie putting up with *three* babies.

"I give them less than a week."

"Excellent!" I was too happy. "When Mom and I came home last night, Chad was passed out on the living room floor. He ate all the cookie dough ice cream. I didn't even get a taste. He eats more than my pregnant sister."

"Those twins will be terrors, but you're going to be a great aunt."

"You really think so?" I tried to imagine my new nephews. I hoped they had Rose Marie's eyes and ambition.

"I know so," AJ reassured.

I smiled at the thought of two little boys dressed in identical clothes. I'd have to get a job just to make sure they had cool wardrobes.

I nearly jumped from my bed at the knocking on my door. My sore head wasn't ready for any sudden noises. "Listen, someone is at my door. See if your mom will let you off house arrest tonight."

"I'm already off."

"Ooooh, you're good," I purred.

"I know," AJ bragged.

"I gotta go."

"Later."

I closed my phone and heaved my tired body out of bed. If AJ hadn't woken me up, I would have slept the whole day. My feet felt like bricks. I slowly trudged toward the door. The nagging knock continued.

I opened to see my sister, looking not at me but at the left side of my face. She was probably enjoying the view.

"What's up?" I leaned my aching head against the doorframe. I wasn't in the mood to deal with Rose Marie.

She smiled smugly and folded her arms across her chest. "You look like crap."

Enough of her attitude! I tried to slam the door in her face, but she blocked it with her elbow.

"Don't shut the door. I didn't mean it to be rude."

Rose Marie pushed her way into my room. "Mom told me what happened last night and I wanted to see if I could offer my services."

"What services?" This was so humiliating. What did she have to offer me other than teasing for the rest of my life?

"I didn't win runner up in Greenwood County Miss Glamour or Greenwood High School Homecoming Queen for nothing." She grabbed my chin and peered closer at my face. "I'm pretty sure I can cover up that bruise."

"Really?" Was Rose Marie here to be nice? Had she called a truce? I hoped so. I was tired of fighting, and besides, I knew my face needed major help. I hadn't looked in the mirror since sitting in the ER last night. I didn't expect to look any better today, especially since the swelling felt worse.

"Sure." Rose Marie walked to my vanity table and unloaded the contents of her cosmetic bag.

"Thanks." I sat in the chair in front of my vanity and when I saw my reflection in the mirror, I screamed.

"Hey," she quipped, "I didn't say this would be easy." She grabbed my knees and turned me around. "Now, I don't want you looking until I am completely finished. An artist must work undisturbed."

After only a few minutes of Rose Marie smearing and brushing cosmetics on my sore face, she was finished.

"Are you ready to look?" She turned me toward the full-length mirror. .

I couldn't believe what I saw. Not only was the bruise concealed, but the way she did my makeup made me look kind of pretty. "I...I can barely notice."

"Not bad, huh?" Rose Marie rested her hand on my shoulder. "You should let me show you how to do your makeup. You've got nice eyes and I know how to bring out your shade of green."

"Really, you'd show me how to look pretty?" Not only would I show up Monday without a bruise, but I'd look better than ever. Rose Marie's artistry wasn't too overdone, like Summer or Marisela, who caked on all the shades of the rainbow. Although Rose Marie picked natural tones for the eye shadow, blush and lipstick, the girl staring back looked more like a movie star than a fat dork.

"Of course," she said. "Like Lu Lu did for me when I was your age."

"Thanks, Rose Marie." Before she could react, I grabbed her in a tight embrace.

"That's what sisters are for." She patted my head before she pulled away and walked toward the bed. Rose Marie sank onto the mattress and covered her bulging stomach with a pillow.

For the first time, I noticed the dark circles under her eyes and her sloppy sweat pants. Rose Marie had always looked perfect. Why didn't she do for herself what she'd done for me? Her brow was creased into a frown and the corners of her lips were turned down.

I couldn't help but feel something was wrong with my sister. "Rose Marie?"

"Yeah." Her head was down now, as she focused on the pillow in her lap.

"I'm sorry we've been fighting."

"Me, too." She looked up and managed a half smile.

I sat beside her and squeezed her hand. "When the babies come, I promise to be a good aunt."

"Babies?" She jerked back, knocking the pillow to the ground. "Hold on, we're only having one."

"Oh, I'm sorry." I bit my bottom lip. "I thought you said you were having twins." Nice save. I couldn't exactly explain my psychic best friend had already predicted two kids.

"Do I look that fat?" Rose Marie ran a hand over her stomach and sat up straight.

"No." But the truth was, she did. Lately, she'd been wearing Chad's sweats and T-shirts. I figured it was to cover her belly, but even under bulky clothes, I could see her round stomach. She resumed her slouch, hand resting on her stomach. "I haven't even been to the doctor yet."

"You haven't?"

"No, Mom is taking me on Monday." Smiling, her eyes lingered on her belly. "I get to hear the baby's heartbeat."

"What if there are two babies?" My gaze traveled to her protruding stomach. I looked for a sign but I couldn't tell. I didn't know what I was expecting. Two heads were not about to pop out and say 'hello'. "Will you hear two heartbeats?"

Rose Marie stopped smiling and tilted her head. "You're not very funny."

I grimaced and shrugged. "I was just wondering."

"I guess so, but trust me, twins don't run in either of our families. We're *not* having twins."

Rose Marie sounded more like she was trying to convince herself than me. Did she have doubts? I focused on her thoughts.

She's right, I'm too fat for three months.

Uh-oh, Rose Marie was in for a big shock. "Well, it's always good to be prepared."

"Sophie," Rose Marie sighed and shook her head. "I'm not even prepared for this one."

Chapter Twelve

Even though I had worried all morning about other kids teasing me about the football incident, I couldn't wait to see if Frankie noticed my new look. My hair was shorter, layered and highlighted with gold and auburn accents. I was also sporting new clothes. The swelling on my face had gone down. All that was left was a barely visible black eye, thanks to Rose Marie and her cosmetic skills.

I felt all eyes upon me as I followed AJ onto the bus. My pace slowed as I inwardly grimaced. Were they staring at me because I looked hot or did they just want to get a peek at the football geek? I couldn't help it. I *had* to know. I willed myself to listen to a few thoughts.

Cute hair.

Wow! She's hot.

Confidence restored, my stride increased when I saw Krysta at the back of the bus. She was waiting, saving the usual seats in front of her for AJ and a spot beside her for me. Her eyelids looked heavy, her makeup a little smudged.

"Hey." AJ threw her backpack on her seat and flung herself onto the bench. "What happened to you this weekend? We tried calling you."

Krysta rubbed her temples and looked through half open eyes. "I was visiting old friends."

"Live ones?" I whispered.

I could see the veins pop in Krysta's neck.

She looked at me and shook her head. "Nope."

"Fun," AJ teased. "All we did was go to the mall."

I gently squeezed her shoulder. "Want to talk about it?"

"Let's just say." Krysta tipped back her head and sank into her seat. "You're not the only one with increasing powers."

AJ hung over the front seat, coming within inches of our personal space. "I guess it's happening to all of us."

Krysta's eyes bulged. "You, too, AJ?"

"Yeah." AJ shrugged. "But I don't understand why now."

I had a theory, but it still didn't make any sense. "Maybe it has something to do with puberty."

AJ rolled her eyes. "Yeah, like our gifts bloom with our budding breasts." She pointed to Krysta's backpack with a magazine poking out of the top of the bag. "Does your *Cosmo* mention anything about bra size and supernatural powers?"

"I'll have to check on that." Krysta turned to me and smiled. "By the way, how are you feeling?"

I covered my eyes and sank into my seat. "You heard?"

"I saw it."

Just great! I wonder how many other people were watching. "I'm so embarrassed."

"Things happen." Krysta patted my shoulder and squinted her eyes. "But I can't even tell you were hit. You look really pretty today."

"Thanks." I cupped my hands under my chin and batted my eyes. "Rose Marie did my makeup."

"So you two are talking now?" Krysta grabbed my hand and placed it on her neck.

"Yeah. We're better." I took the hint and rubbed the knots on Krysta's neck and back.

"She still with the loser?" Krysta rolled her head back and closed her eyes.

"Yeah." I smirked. "But AJ says not for long."

"Nice," Krysta softly spoke while keeping her eyes closed. "Not to change the subject, but how are things going with Jacob?"

"You didn't change the subject." I rubbed harder then let go. Jacob was still a sore subject with me. Not because I was offended anymore, but because I felt stupid for ever liking him. "Chad's a loser, Jacob's a loser. I've ditched that crush."

"Excellent." Krysta shook off her limbs and sat up. "Anyone new on the horizon?"

"Maybe." I tucked my chin into my chest. I didn't

want anyone on the bus to overhear gossip about something that hadn't happened yet. Even though I didn't doubt AJ's psychic ability, Frankie still had to ask me to the dance.

AJ leaned even closer and cupped her hands around her mouth. "Frankie Salas is going to ask her to Freshmen Formal."

"Get out!" Krysta punched my arm. "How do you know this?"

AJ cleared her throat. "I saw it coming." She jerked her thumb at me and rolled her eyes. "Sophie still doesn't know if she's going."

Krysta's bottom lip fell. "Are you insane?"

My shoulders sagged. "I heard Summer saying he's going to ask her."

Krysta crossed her legs beneath her, sitting on her heels. She grasped the back of AJ's seat and turned. "You don't believe that, do you?"

"That's what I told her," AJ said.

"It's not just that. Look, every girl likes Frankie. Can you imagine what that dance would be like? I'd be fighting off groupies the whole time." What if Frankie flirted with other girls and ignored me?

AJ turned her gaze down. "Afraid you won't measure up to them?"

Under the scrutiny of my friends, I shifted in my seat. "No, it's not that." When he tutored me in Mrs. Stein's class, I wanted to melt in my seat at his touch, his scent, his nearness. The boy had cast a spell over me and I didn't trust myself not to act like an idiot in his presence.

Krysta squeezed my shoulder. "You're not a fat dork anymore."

"Yeah, Frankie obviously sees something in you," AJ said. "Maybe you should, too."

All this time I'd been trying so hard to prove I was cool. Now that Frankie was interested in me, I was afraid I wouldn't live up to my new image. What if I said something stupid on our date? What if he no longer thought I was cool? Plus, I had another big problem. A problem normal teenagers didn't have to deal with. With Frankie so near me, what if I read something in his mind

I didn't want to know?

****

The bus *had* to be late this morning. Obviously, the substitute bus driver didn't know I had a schedule to keep when he took three wrong turns. I had barely enough time to get to my locker before first period.

But there was just one problem.

"Hey, Sophie, I saw you knocked out on the football field. Actually, the whole school saw it." Summer smirked while she stroked her fake nails with hot pink polish. Her hand was splayed flat against my locker door.

Knowing she had no intention of moving it, I took a deep breath, dropped my book bag to the ground and prepared to do battle. This was a long time coming. I was finally ready to stand up to Summer Powers. Then why were my knees shaking?

"So what's your point?"

The bite of my best friend's angry voice resonated behind me. I turned to see AJ glaring at Summer, chin raised, fists clenched at her sides. Now *she* was ready to do battle. AJ's powerful energy swept over me; I felt her rage in my bones. AJ at my back made me feel safer; my knees stopped shaking.

"Nothing," Summer stammered. "I was just making an observation." She quickly put the cap on her nail polish and stuffed it into her purse.

"Really?" AJ crossed her arms over her chest. "You were staring at someone other than your own reflection?"

"Yeah." Summer's hands were trembling as she snatched a notebook from her locker and slammed the door.

AJ threw back her head and laughed. "Good for you. Maybe this means you'll be spending less time at your locker mirror, so my best friend won't be late to class."

Summer hurried to the opposite end of the hall, but not before casting me a sideways glare. I read the intention in her eyes and heard what she was thinking.

Just you wait. She won't always be there to protect you.

"AJ." I shook my head. "One of these days I'm going to have to learn to stand up for myself."

"You will next time." AJ put her hand on my back. "I

just wanted to show you how it's done."

"Thanks." I fumbled with the combination on my locker.

AJ looked from side to side before lowering her voice. "Did you get to hear what she was thinking?"

I opened my locker, shielding my face with the door. "She can't wait to get me alone."

AJ pushed next to me, pretending to get books out of my locker. "I'm no bigger than you, Sophie. The only difference is I don't take crap from anyone. Next time you see Summer, give her the stare, and show her you're not afraid."

I paused. "And what if she kicks my butt?"

"She might." AJ stopped fumbling and turned to me. "And *you* might kick *her* butt. The point is, you'll have to deal with girls like Summer all your life. Are you going to keep taking their crap?"

I squared my shoulders. "No."

"Now, next time she starts something, get in her face, and then listen to what she's thinking. I will bet you'll find out she's scared."

"Maybe." I wasn't so sure. Could AJ be right? There was only one way to find out. I shuddered at the thought of a future confrontation. If I did get my butt kicked by Summer, the whole school would talk about it. I'd never be cool.

We exchanged knowing glances at the sound of the first bell. AJ waved as she headed to class.

I closed my locker and picked up my bag, anxious to get to first period. AJ told me Frankie scored the winning touchdown Friday night. I hoped Lara got the picture.

"Hey, Sophie, you okay?"

My spine tingled at the sound of the familiar voice behind me. I clenched both fists then breathed out, trying to ease my tension. I knew when I turned around, those penetrating eyes would have me stammering like an idiot. I slowly faced Frankie. "What? Yeah, I'm fine."

He was leaning one hand against Summer's locker, his other hand holding a binder to his chest and head tilted to the side. His gorgeous pose could have been ripped from a GAP ad.

"Oh, when you didn't show up to tutoring, I thought

94

you had a concussion." Frankie smiled slyly, his eyes twinkling with something that looked like arrogance.

This guy was a player, baiting me with his hot body. Did he think I was going to drop to my knees and beg for forgiveness? "Why? Does a girl have to have a concussion if she doesn't want to be with you?"

Frankie pushed off the locker, his shoulders falling slightly. *Damn. That cut hard. I knew she didn't like me.*

Frankie's thoughts stunned me into silence. Had I actually hurt Frankie Salas? I hadn't thought guys like him could be hurt.

Head cast down, Frankie brushed past me. "That's not what I meant. Never mind."

Instinctively, I reached out for his arm. My fingers tingled as I felt his muscles tighten. "Frankie, I'm sorry. I can't believe I said that."

Frankie turned abruptly, closing only a small distance between us.

I released my grip before his skin melted my fingers and tried to turn down the heat that coursed through me when I looked into his eyes. "We had a new bus driver. We just got to school."

"That's okay." A slight smile tugged at the corner of his mouth. "Maybe tomorrow."

"Yeah." I bit my lip. I didn't want a goofy grin ruining the moment. "Definitely."

His eyes locked with mine as he placed his hand on my shoulder. Thinking he was drawing me closer for a kiss, I leaned in. I could feel my mouth dry up like I'd just swallowed a mouthful of cotton. My hands shook, my heart beat so hard I thought my chest would explode, but I didn't care. Frankie Salas was about to kiss me. I closed my eyes and opened my lips...ready, waiting.

"Which way are you going?"

"Huh?" I watched as Frankie slid my book bag off my arm. He wasn't going to kiss me. He was just taking my bag. I was a moron.

"I said, 'which way are you going?'" He had my book bag slung over his shoulder, gripping it with one finger.

"Yearbook," I stammered, the dryness in my mouth almost causing me to choke.

"I'll walk you."

We both turned, walking shoulder to shoulder.

I ran my tongue over the roof of my mouth. "Won't you be late?"

"I don't get busted," Frankie teased. "My teachers love me."

We walked the rest of the way in silence. This gave me ample time to reflect on my stupidity. I just couldn't act cool around Frankie. The weird thing was that he didn't seem to care.

The tardy bell rang. I looked at Frankie to gage his reaction, but he didn't even blink. Although Mrs. Carr wouldn't be happy when I came in late, that didn't seem to matter to me at the time.

When we neared the door to the yearbook room, I knew I had to bring up the football incident, as Frankie was nice enough not to mention it. "Frankie, thanks for everything Friday night."

He shrugged, setting down my bag. "It's nothing."

"I heard you still won the game."

"Yeah." He held up a finger. "By one point."

I sighed, sinking against the door. "I wish I could have seen you make that touchdown."

He moved closer. "There's always this Friday."

I inhaled his scent. Fresh, musky, and not a hint of ketchup.

"Maybe I can get a picture of you." I could feel the butterflies fluttering in my stomach. I'd misjudged his last move. I didn't know what to expect now so I wasn't going to make that same mistake again. I tried to focus on his thoughts, but with my nerves and his dark eyes, there was no hope of any mind-reading.

He placed one hand above my shoulder, leaning against the door, his face within inches of mine. "Or the Friday after that."

My mind was racing. Frankie's nearness had me so confused. It took me a few seconds to register what he was saying. He didn't have a game that Friday. That was the night of the Freshmen Formal dance. "I thought you didn't have a game that Friday." I nearly stumbled over my words.

"I don't." He grabbed a wisp of my hair, toying it in his fingers, his breath lowering to a near whisper. "So maybe you and I can get some pictures together."

I tried to swallow, but the dryness in my throat was back with a vengeance. I looked into his penetrating eyes, searching for a sign this wasn't a dream, the hottest guy in school really liked me. "Like, as friends?"

"No, as dates." He leaned closer.

I smelled his minty breath and saw his lips part. I knew Frankie Salas was going to kiss me.

"The bell rang a minute ago," a gruff voice said. "Get to class, you kids, before I write you up."

I jumped at the sight of Tyler, the gender confused rent-a-cop.

Frankie slowly straightened, turning to Tyler with a wide grin. "Oh, hi, Tyler. You look beautiful this morning. New haircut?"

Beautiful? Feminine term. Finally, the riddle was solved. Tyler was a girl.

Tyler blushed and playfully swatted her hand at him. "Frankie, you little rascal, get your butt to class."

"Yes, Ma'am." Frankie was a player. He even knew how to make the beastie girls blush. "I was just making sure Sophie didn't pass out on the way to class. She got a concussion at the game."

"Oh, so you're the one who was hit by the ball." She peered around his shoulder and looked me up and down with a menacing glare.

I tried to duck behind Frankie. "Uh, yeah." Even though I had solved Tyler's gender enigma, two hundred fifty pounds of grudge with a night stick was still scary.

"I saw the whole thing from the sidelines." She grunted and puffed up her chest. "Girls don't belong on the football field, that's what I've always said."

I felt like saying, "So what the heck are *you*? A few seconds ago, Frankie had me convinced *you* were a girl."

A few seconds before that, Frankie was about to kiss me. But she, he or it, had to ruin the moment.

****

Mrs. Carr glared from underneath her rimmed glasses as I floated into the yearbook room and melted into the seat next to Lara.

She was adjusting contrast on photos of screaming cheerleaders. "Mrs. Carr is sending the pep rally pages this deadline. Open up the folder on the network and pick your ten favorite pictures."

"Sure."

I opened up the folder, vaguely aware I was looking at pictures of kids with pie on their faces. Then I came to a group of football players throwing water on their coach. Frankie was holding the bucket. He had that mischievous twinkle in his eyes. He would make a fun date, especially to the Freshmen Formal. The thought of us on the dance floor together brought a smile to my face.

"Sophie?" Lara bit her lip and looked at me questioningly, "Jacob put you in a good mood?"

"Oh, God, no!" I sat up and shuttered, making a disgusting face.

Lara smiled and nodded. "Well, that's good to know."

"Jacob's a loser," I huffed.

"I'm glad you see it." She cast me a sideways glance. "Took you long enough."

I felt like a complete idiot. How could Lara have stayed friends with me when I was such a mental case over a loser? Maybe now she'd tell me the whole truth. "Now that I'm through with him, you gonna tell me what he did to you?"

Lara pushed her shoulders back and narrowed her eyes. "You mean you never heard the rumors?"

"No." Did everyone know Jacob was a vomit heap but me? I guess everyone, except AJ, decided to let me learn the truth on my own.

"Remember when I was crying in the darkroom?" Lara whispered.

"Yeah." I wanted to pretend I didn't remember, but that day had been difficult to put from my mind. Even though I didn't want to believe what she was thinking, that was the first day I started having doubts about Jacob.

"Jacob had just told everyone on my bus I had sex with him." Lara rolled her eyes. "I don't even know him."

"What a jerk. Why didn't you tell me?" She did tell me and now I was silently kicking myself in the butt for not wanting to believe her thoughts. Jacob had insulted my friend. I should have ditched that crush on the spot.

"You're my only friend right now. Everyone else

thinks I'm a slut thanks to Summer and Jacob." Lara sank in her seat, lines of doubt drawn across her forehead. "I didn't want you to hate me, too."

"Lara." I squeezed her hand. "I wouldn't hate you."

"I don't know." She wagged her finger at my nose. "You were pretty lovesick over Jacob."

"Uugghh, don't remind me." I laid my hand across my forehead. If I could have erased those weeks. Stupid, stupid, stupid.

"So who's the new crush?" Lara playfully punched me on the shoulder, her eyes twinkling with mischief.

What a good friend. How easily she forgave and forgot my bad taste in guys. After all, it was not like I married the guy. Besides, I had better prospects on the horizon. "Frankie Salas. He asked me to Freshmen Formal. He almost kissed me this morning, but The Beast ruined it."

"Frankie Salas?" Lara squeezed her hands between her knees and batted her eyes. "Oh, Sophie, he's a hottie…and so sweet."

I frowned. "So I've heard from every other girl in this school."

"So what? Just think, all those girls like him but he picked you." Lara nearly fell out of her seat in excitement.

"You're right, but…" I bit my thumb, shaking my head. So many girls.

"But?" Lara tilted her head, raising her brows as if waiting for me to finish. "Sophie?"

"I just don't want to be fighting over him all night, that's all." I didn't see myself in his league, and definitely not with so many pretty girls competing for his attention.

Lara turned up her chin. "Frankie's not a jerk like Jacob. If Frankie wants something, he goes for it. If he wants to take you to the dance, you won't be fighting over him. He'll be all yours."

Even though he did have a lot of female followers, Frankie had something about his character I liked. Like how he worked so hard in football, how he did so well in school, and how he made me feel with the cute way he teased me. But how did Lara know so much about him? I didn't want to add Lara to my list of rivals. "How do *you* know so much about him?"

Lara cast a sideways smile that shot to her eyes. She must have sensed my jealously. "I've got him in five classes and I've been taking his football pictures for three years. When Frankie focuses on something, it's like nothing else exists. Besides, I saw how worried he was when he carried you off the field Friday night."

An honest, nice guy who liked me? It didn't add up. "I just don't get it."

"Don't get what, Sophie?"

"Why me?" Why me when he had hundreds of girls to chose from?

Lara sighed. "Does this have anything to do with that chubby picture of you from the seventh grade?"

"I was a dork, Lara. Didn't you see me?" The memories of my seventh grade year came flooding back, forming a tight knot in my chest. 'So Fat Sinora', 'Eats-A-Pizza Sinora', 'Cellulite Sinora'. I didn't even know what cellulite was until seventh grade when Cody Miller pointed at my thighs in front our entire geography class.

"People change, Sophie." Lara rested her hand on my shoulder. "Frankie sees that, why can't you?"

I put my head down, trying to repress the tears, as my throat tightened. "They called me 'So Fat'."

"Kids are mean. How'd you like to be labeled the school slut? It's a lot easier for *you* to change *your* image than it is for *me* to get some respect." Lara's voice rose a few octaves as she turned her head.

Poor Lara. The hottest guy in school asked me to Freshmen Formal and I thought I was having a bad day. Her life was much worse. "I'd never thought of that. I'm sorry, Lara."

"It's okay." She quickly brushed the corner of her eyes with the back of her hand. "I'm used to it. Listen, promise me you'll go with him because if you don't, I'm never talking to you again. Just think about it, you're my only friend so I'll be losing a lot, too."

****

"Okay." Mrs. Stein scanned the room with a subdued smile that didn't quite mask the sadness in her eyes. "Open your books to page seventy-two. I want you to do all the practice equations."

I looked at the equations. Funny, they didn't seem so

challenging now. With enough work, and maybe the right tutor, I knew I could pass math.

"Sophie." Mrs. Stein kneeled beside my desk and spoke in a low whisper. "Where were you this morning?"

"The bus was late."

She clicked her tongue and shook her head. "Frankie Salas waited all morning for you." Her voice rose just loud enough to be dangerous.

"Really?" I squeezed the pages of my book and beamed. I had the boy hooked.

Students in nearby desks began whispering and looking at me. They must have overheard us.

"Sophie likes Frankie Salas." Cody Miller yelled to no one in particular.

Mrs. Stein rose and glared in his direction. "Hush, Cody, that's none of your business."

Many students quietly laughed and snickered.

Scanning the room, Mrs. Stein threw her hands in the air. "Leave the poor girl alone and get to work. I swear some days you kids have me at wits end."

Grody Cody stuck out his chin, smirking. "But you know you love us, Mrs. Stein."

"Yeah." She sighed and shook her head. "You know I do."

"Mrs. Stein." Cody chewed on the tip of his eraser, lost in thought.

I held my breath. I never knew what was going to come out of that boy's mouth. He was known to say totally off the wall, weird things. Hopefully, he'd forgotten about Frankie Salas and me.

Cody stopped chewing and a light went on in those dim eyes. "Why don't you have your own kids?"

I knew it was a rude question so I wasn't shocked Cody had asked it. Curiosity got the best of me as I waited among the silent audience for the answer.

Oh, God, why didn't I die with them? I just want to die.

As Mrs. Stein's painful thoughts projected into my brain, an overwhelming, numbing pain washed over me, sinking my spirit into a chasm so deep, I felt my soul encompassed in pure, depressing darkness. I knew I was not just listening to her thoughts, I had entered Mrs.

Stein's soul. Who died? And now she wanted to die, too? Not my favorite teacher!

She clutched her book so fiercely, I thought she would crush it. Her eyes welled up with tears, but she didn't say a word as she quickly walked out of the room.

The class waited in silence, but she didn't return.

"What'd you open your big mouth for, Cody?" AJ sneered.

Cody cowered and whined, "What? What'd I say?"

"Her family is dead, Cody."

I gasped at the sound of The Beast's harsh voice. I hadn't even heard Tyler enter the room.

Tyler glared at us from the back of the classroom, arms folded across its chest. "You kids shut your mouths and get back to work. I'm watching you while your teacher cools down."

My heart sank into my stomach, as I closed my eyes trying to understand what had just happened. Mrs. Stein was a great teacher who loved us. She didn't deserve this. She was depressed because her family died and I seemed to be the only one who knew the depths of her inner turmoil. She needed help, but I couldn't help her if she didn't willingly tell me. No adult would believe me if I said, "Mrs. Stein's thoughts said she wishes she was dead." They'd get me the shrink, not her.

****

The incident with Mrs. Stein kind of shadowed my excitement about Frankie. I thought about my favorite teacher all day, even when Frankie flirted with me in English. He probably thought I was playing hard to get. I hoped not. I didn't want him to think I was some annoying little tease.

I needed to get home, so I could have some privacy. I couldn't really think about Mrs. Stein's problems until I was sure no one else's thoughts would pop into my head. In the meantime, I had the bus ride to face. I was sure AJ and Krysta wanted to know if Frankie had asked me to the dance.

They were already waiting for me on the bus. Their wide-eyed expressions said it all. They wanted me to spill the news.

I couldn't suppress a laugh as I scanned their eager

faces. "He asked me."

AJ slapped the back of her seat and yelped. "You said 'yes' I hope."

I shook my head. "The Beast interrupted us."

"You'd better say 'yes'," Krysta squealed.

"Okay, I'll go." I sighed and tilted the back of my head against the seat. "I guess I'll have to fight off his groupies all night."

AJ folded her arms across the top of her seat and looked into my eyes. "What's your plan?"

I raised my chin up, keeping my voice firm. "I need to show all Greenwood girls I won't take any crap, starting with Summer Powers."

"Awesome." AJ nodded approval. "You're learning."

"How are you going to do that?" Krysta didn't sound sure of my plan.

I shrugged. "I don't know yet."

AJ balled her fist into her hand. "You need to throw the first punch."

I grimaced. "That's what I'm thinking."

Krysta shook her head. "You'll be suspended, and then Sparks won't allow you at the dance."

Krysta was right. I'd never considered myself much of a fighter, anyway. I needed to catch Summer off guard. But how? Suddenly, I had a revelation and I sprung from my seat. "Wait a minute! First punches don't always have to be physical."

AJ raised her brows. "You gonna clue us in?"

My mind was racing. I had a lot to do to prepare for the first punch. All I needed was some tape, some courage, and Lara's cooperation. My plan could work. It *had* to work.

I focused my gaze on my friends, smiling as it all came together in my head. "It's a surprise. Don't you wish *you* were mind readers?"

Chapter Thirteen

Finally, alone. I threw my bag on the floor and flopped onto the bed, rubbing my aching temples. So much to think about. So much to plan. Mrs. Stein, Frankie, Summer—they were all running through my head and I didn't know where to begin.

"Hey." Rose Marie stood in the open doorway.

I looked at my sister, annoyed I'd forgotten to shut the door. "Hey."

Rose Marie put her head down, squeezing the door frame. "I kicked him out."

I couldn't believe what I was hearing. My sister had come to her senses. I had thought she was hopeless. "What?"

A single tear slipped down her cheek. "He decided he's not ready to be a father."

For the first time, I felt sorry for her. I had been an idiot over a guy once, too, although I never let my crush go nearly as far. Still, she was my sister and needed my support. "Are you okay?"

"I'm fine." She managed a half-smile. "Never been better."

I crossed my arms over my chest and narrowed my gaze. "You don't sound better."

"Well, you were right." Keeping her head down, she ran a hand over her belly. "I am fat for three months."

"I never said that."

Rose Marie looked up, more tears began to flow. "There were two heartbeats, Sophie."

I didn't know what to say. She obviously wasn't happy, so I couldn't congratulate her.

She wiped her cheeks with the back of her hand. "How am I going to raise two babies?"

I tried to sound reassuring. "You've got us to help you."

She sat on the bed and placed her head in her hands. "What was I thinking, Sophie?"

"Love is blind, I guess." Unfortunately, I knew what I was talking about.

"No, love is stupid." She stood up and paced the room. "I thought I'd be able to finish college after the baby. I had all these crazy ideas. Now I'll be stuck with a minimum wage job, living with my parents, raising two kids with no father." She turned, pointing an accusing finger. "Don't be stupid and screw up your life like I did, Sophie."

"I don't plan on it."

"So." She threw her hands in the air and rolled her eyes. "How was your day?"

I bit my lip. I didn't know if she'd be eager to share my good news. "Frankie Salas, the hottest guy in school, asked me to the Freshmen Formal."

"That's great!" Rose Marie patted my knee. "Look at my little sister, growing up so fast." She glared at me. "This guy had better have ambition."

I shook my head, laughing. "I'm not marrying him, Rose Marie."

"Good, don't marry until you finish college." Her face twisted while she looked me over. "So why the long face when you came home?"

"You noticed?" I sighed and laid back, folding my hands behind my head.

"Yeah, even though I seem focused on only my problems lately, I still pay attention when my sister comes home with a frown, dragging her feet."

I rolled over, clutching my pillow. "Do you remember Mrs. Stein?"

Rose Marie smiled. "Mrs. Stein? If it wasn't for her, I don't think I'd have scored a 1500 on my SATs. She was my favorite teacher ever."

I sat up. "Mine, too." Maybe Rose Marie could help me with Mrs. Stein. I didn't have to tell her all the mind reading details.

"How's she doing?" Rose Marie leaned in and lowered her voice, as if she was about to leak top-secret information. "She lost her family, you know?"

My shoulders fell. This was the second time I'd heard the bad news and it didn't get any easier. "Yeah, I heard.

She's been pretty depressed, Rose Marie. I'm worried about her."

"Really?"

"Yeah. What exactly happened to her family?"

Rose Marie bit her nails. Something she only did when she was in a really serious mood. "Her husband and kids died in a car wreck a few summers ago. It was really bad. I heard her youngest daughter survived for a few weeks, but she was brain dead. They had to pull the plug."

Brain dead? That's why she got so upset when I told her I was brain dead at tutoring. This was bad. This was worse than bad. What a horrible thing to happen to my favorite teacher! "Was she in the car?"

"No, she was at some teachers' retreat up in the mountains. They were going to pick her up when their car went over a cliff."

"That sucks." I slowly exhaled, trying to process this new information. Was this why she was so overprotective of her students? Why she became distraught when Tyler tried to snatch one of her 'babies'? She wasn't in the car to save her babies, so she was intent on saving all of her students. It made sense, in a morbid sort of way.

"She was still teaching eighth grade math. I was in high school when it happened." She grabbed a tissue off my nightstand and blew her nose. "I went to visit her, but they said she took the year off. Some kids said she was in a mental hospital. *But* you know how kids lie."

"Yeah." I rested my chin on the pillow. "I know."

"Anyway, I never got back to thank her for everything she did for me. I was too wrapped up in that loser." *I can't believe how many people I'd neglected when I was with him.*

Hearing my sister's thoughts, I looked up to see she'd started crying again. She was hunched over, her forehead resting in her hands.

I leaned over and rubbed her back. "It's too late to change the past, but maybe you can stop by and visit her. I'm sure it would make her feel good to see an old student. She could use a boost."

"You're right." She perked up. "Maybe I'll stop by tomorrow morning. My morning sickness is easing up."

"Great. You can drive me to school. Our bus driver made me late to class today and I missed tutoring with Frankie."

"Ooohhh." She swatted my shoulder. "So I get to see Mrs. Stein *and* the hottest guy in school."

"Yeah." I cringed at the thought of my sister teasing me or Frankie. "But could you do me a favor?"

"What?"

I looked at her through the corner of my eyes. "Don't say anything to make me look stupid."

"Would I do something like that?" Rose Marie gasped and batted her lashes.

Yeah, she would but Rose Marie was the least of my worries. I had worse trouble than an embarrassing big sister. If my plan worked though…my problem would be solved. Tomorrow morning, I planned to throw the first punch.

Chapter Fourteen

"Sophie, what took you so long?" Hands on hips, Rose Marie stood at the front of Mrs. Stein's classroom. "I thought you would just be gone for a minute."

Rose Marie, Mrs. Stein and Frankie were waiting for me in the classroom, although by the looks of it, they weren't missing me too much. I had walked in just as Frankie and Mrs. Stein had burst into laughter. Something my wicked sister had said, no doubt.

"Sorry." I shrugged, trying to shake off my nervousness. "I had to stop off at my locker."

Actually, I did more than stop off. Summer hadn't made it to her locker yet, so I had time to carry out my plan. I tried not to look at what I'd done as revenge. Even though it felt good to know that soon Summer would be the laughing stock of the entire school.

"That's okay. We've been keeping Frankie company while you've been gone." Rose Marie laughed. "I've been telling him *lots* of stories about your childhood."

My childhood? Was she telling him about the fat me? I felt like I should have been alarmed but somehow that didn't matter anymore. "Thanks." I rolled my eyes and gave my sister a warning glare. "I'm sorry, Frankie."

"That's okay." He was sitting on top of a desk in a casual pose, looking just as hot as ever.

"Rose Marie, why don't I take you into the staff lounge?" Mrs. Stein said between laughs while pressing her palms against her ribs. "Mr. Dallin is subbing here. He still talks about you. I bet he'd love to see you." Mrs. Stein's eyes lit upon my sister.

They locked arms and headed toward the door. Well, if it made Mrs. Stein happy, it was worth it to see her laughing at my expense.

"Okay, we'll leave you two alone to your...uh...equations." Rose Marie deliberately bumped against my shoulder as she walked past.

"Go away." I made a mental note to clean my toilet with her toothbrush when I got home.

"So." Frankie grabbed the tips of my fingers and gently placed them in his hands. "What's the answer?"

The shock of his touch sent shivers through me, but I was starting to figure out Frankie Salas and having a lot of fun doing it. "Answer to what?" I batted my eyes.

He instantly released my hand. *You bonehead. She doesn't want to go with you. Just drop it.* "Uh, nevermind."

Listening to his insecurities and instantly missing his touch, I reached for his hand. "Do you mean that equation you taught me?"

He gently squeezed and moved closer. "Yeah."

I bit my lip, smiling. "I've been thinking about that equation all night."

"You have?" His chest rose.

"I think I came up with a better one."

"What is it?" He whispered.

Afraid to break the spell, I inched closer. "$S + F = FF$. Now imagine S stands for a girl and F stands for a guy. What dance do you know has the initials FF?"

He laughed, cupping my chin in his hand. "This is why I like you, Sophie."

His soft touch turned me into butter. I wanted to melt into his arms. "Why?"

"Because you're you," he said softly, "that's why."

"Well, in that case." I looked into his amber eyes, wanting nothing more than a kiss from the hottest guy in school. "We need to get some pictures together next Friday."

He pulled my chin toward his lips and bent down for a kiss. "What was that?" Frankie jerked his head up.

The shrill scream of the meanest teen in the school echoed through the halls and broke our spell. Of all the rotten luck.

I groaned. "I think it was a girl screaming."

Frankie pulled me toward the door. "Maybe we should check it out."

I pulled back, digging my heels into the pasty yellow school tiles. "It's probably nothing." Which was a lie, but I had two very important reasons for staying put. First of all, I didn't want to blow my second chance to get a kiss from Frankie. Secondly, I didn't want to get my butt kicked.

Suddenly, I started to have major doubts. Yeah, I knew Summer would be furious when she went to her locker. I knew by playing this prank, I would be forced to confront her. But after listening to her angry scream, which was still reverberating in my ears and down to my toes, I wondered if throwing the first punch was actually a good idea.

"It doesn't sound like nothing." He opened the door, dragging me behind. "Come on!"

****

Summer crumpled the infamous booger pick picture in her hand. The corners of the picture were still stuck to her locker, thanks to lots and lots of duct tape.

"Where is Lara?" Summer was scanning the faces of the amused crowd. "I know she did this! I'll kill her!"

I whispered to Frankie that I had something to take care of before pushing my way to the front. The first punch had been thrown. It was time to see if she'd strike back.

Taking a deep breath, I straightened my spine while trying to control my shaking legs. "Lara didn't do it, Summer. I did." I inwardly smiled after the words came out of my mouth. I was terrified, but it felt so good to finally stand up for myself.

Summer's jaw dropped, her eyes bugging out of her head. "You?" she hissed.

"Yeah, me." I fisted my hands at my sides, a defiant gesture AJ had taught me. "So what are you going to do about it?"

It was like someone else was speaking. I could barely feel my lips moving, as my body had gone numb. As a voice in my head kept repeating, 'Don't back down,' I realized my next move. Willing myself to read Summer's mind, I wasn't about to be unprepared for Summer's attack.

Sophie? No way! Where did she get the nerve? Summer glared at the gathering crowd. "What are you all laughing at?"

Perfect. Summer was shocked and embarrassed. As

my confidence restored, so did the feeling in my limbs. I decided to strike again before she regained her footing. "I think they're laughing at that picture of you with your finger halfway up your nose."

"You stupid little freak!" She threw the picture in my face as her lower lip trembled.

I caught the picture, laughing, and unfolded it. "Pick-N-Flick Powers—sounds like a cool nickname." Once again, I focused on her thoughts.

Why isn't she backing down? She's gone crazy. "Give that back." Summer lunged for the picture.

I tossed it on the ground. "Sure. I have a hard copy." I was having fun humiliating her, but I had to be cautious. She was a cornered animal; I wasn't sure if she'd strike out. Luckily, her thoughts came easily to me.

Summer picked up the picture, stuffing it in her pocket. Her body quivered as she eyed the crowd. *Everyone's looking. I need to save face.* "I'll get you back for this."

"Yeah, whatever." I folded my arms across my chest and pretended to examine my fingernails. A trick I'd seen her use. "I've got lots more pictures. Don't think I won't print them, or I could always post them on My Space."

She backed up a few steps, her chest rising and falling with each angry breath. "You'd better watch your back."

"You'd better watch your mouth." Jerking my head up, I pointed an irate finger and followed her retreat. "Quit spreading lies about Lara. And when I need to get into my locker, stay out of my face."

What's wrong with her? I have to get out of here. Summer turned, pushing her way through the crowd just as the first bell rang. "You're lucky the bell rang," she called over her shoulder.

I laughed as she ran to class. I couldn't help adding one more jab. "Maybe I'll see you around after first period. Just remember to use antibacterial lotion before you come near my locker."

"Summer Powers piss you off?"

I turned to see Frankie behind me, holding my bookbag.

Putting Summer down was like a drug for my ego; I

still hadn't come off of my high. "I was tired of her crap."

"Yeah." He shrugged. "I've noticed she starts stuff with all the pretty girls."

My chest tightened and I had to remind myself to breathe. Frankie thought I was pretty. The fat little dork had come a long way and hearing him say it made it so much better. My head swelled. I understood how Frankie could get so cocky. Even though he liked me, something still had been bothering me for the past few weeks. "Summer said you were going to ask her to the Freshmen Formal."

"Yeah, right," Frankie laughed. "She's been begging me to take her ever since school started." He winked and grabbed my hand. "Let's go before we're late to class again."

****

"Nice job. I didn't even need to cheat for you." Jacob's fingers slid across mine as he handed back my test.

I wanted to gag. What did I ever see in this guy? "It's called studying, Jacob."

Jacob's eyebrows wrinkled, and then he smiled. "I heard what you did to Summer. Cool."

"Cool?" I pushed back my shoulders, trying to sound as sarcastic as possible. "That's nice. Why don't you play your game boy?"

Jacob's mouth fell open and he waited before sneering. "What crawled up your butt?"

I laughed, looking him in the eyes. "You did."

"What did I do to you?"

I narrowed my eyes, giving him my best 'you're an idiot' smile. "Lara Sketchum."

"Whatever." He shook his head and turned. *She deserved it. She's a slut.*

Ooohhh, what a jerk. His thought was too rude to leave unanswered. "She's not a slut, Jacob. She's my friend and you spread lies about her. Even if she was a slut, she wouldn't get together with a loser who only plays video games."

Jacob faced me again, his upper lip curled into a fierce snarl. "Are you calling me a loser?"

Unimpressed, I rolled my eyes. "You caught on fast."

Jacob leaned back and forced a laugh, dramatically

shrugging his shoulders as if he wasn't bothered. "I thought you were cool, but I take it back."

"I think she's cool." Frankie glared at Jacob with a steely gaze.

Jacob's voice lowered, faltering as he spoke. "Stay out of it, Frankie."

"Too bad. I'm in it." He continued glaring at Jacob.

Jacob turned, huffing as he slammed his Gameboy on his desk, tuning out the rest of the world.

I was so totally proud of Frankie. He told off his friend for me. I'd never thought the guy could get any hotter.

Frankie leaned over as we passed our tests to the front of the room. "I never got your number."

I held out my hand. "Give me your phone."

Within seconds, I entered my number into his phone and I resisted the urge to scan his phonebook. If he had other girls' numbers, it wasn't my business. After all, I reminded myself, I wasn't looking to marry the guy.

Deftly slipping Frankie the cell, I fought the urge to jump out of my seat when his electrified fingers glided over mine. I didn't think I could ever get used to his touch.

He slipped the phone into his pocket. "I'll text you next period."

I slid down in my seat, melting. I still couldn't believe I was going to the Freshman Formal with the coolest guy in school. "Okay." The dance was less than two weeks away; Frankie and I needed to make plans. I didn't think, in all my fourteen years, I'd ever wanted anything more than for that night to finally come. If only everyone else in my life could have been this happy.

Chapter Fifteen

Walking home from the bus stop, I spied Rose Marie in the front yard. She was piling clothes into the back of her SUV. That sight worried me. Had Dad kicked her out? Was she going back to Chad?

"Good news, Sophie." Grinning, Rose Marie grabbed a lamp from off the ground and set it on top of the clothes. "You get your room back."

That much I could tell. But what would happen to my sister and my nephews? "Where are you going?"

Rose Marie paused to rub her lower back. "I'm going to finish my core classes at Central Community."

"Central Community? I didn't know they had dorms."

"They don't." She shrugged. "But Mrs. Stein lives a few blocks away."

"You're moving in with Mrs. Stein?" I couldn't believe my ears. When had this happened? Sure, I noticed Rose Marie was spending a lot more time with her after school, but roommates?

"Yeah. She's been helping me with student loans and scholarships. When the babies come, I'll go to school at night while she watches them."

I felt a pang of jealousy. How was Mrs. Stein going to have the time to do all this and be my favorite teacher? "Wow. That's a lot of work for her."

"That's what I said, but she insisted." Rose Marie picked up another lamp, and then turned. "You know, I think she needs me as much as I need her."

"I think you're right." I shouldn't have been jealous. My plan to cheer Mrs. Stein worked better than I'd hoped. She would have a family again.

"She already found me a job working at her friend's daycare, so I can be with the babies at work. Besides," Rose Marie grinned. "The daycare will be good experience, since I'm going to be a teacher."

My sister was full of surprises. I would have never guessed she wanted to be a teacher. She'd wanted to be a doctor since before college. "You are? Why?" I didn't try to mask the shock in my voice.

"Mom and Dad always expected me to be a doctor like Lu Lu." Rose Marie's head dropped. "After I had Mrs. Stein in eighth grade, I wanted to be a teacher. To help kids the way she helped me."

I felt more than just a sisterly connection with Rose Marie. It was surprising to know we shared the same views, too. "Yeah, Mrs. Stein makes me feel that way."

Her eyes lit and she came over, squeezing my shoulder. "Anyway, she is getting the babies' room ready as we speak. Wait until you see her tomorrow, Sophie. I'll bet you've never seen her so happy."

"I can't wait." For once in my life, everything was coming together. Summer didn't bother me after the pick incident. Jacob was told to shut up. Frankie thought I was pretty. Rose Marie was getting her life back on track. And now, Mrs. Stein would finally have some happiness. The only thing that could top this was a memorable Freshmen Formal.

****

The night was already going better than hoped, except for that one little incident when Rose Marie drove us to the dance. She complimented Frankie about his gorgeous eyes and flirtatious Frankie actually turned beet red. I couldn't wait till I got my driver's license. Dates would be so much better.

Thank God for those dance lessons Mom made me take in seventh grade. Even though I was the fattest thing in spandex, I still learned a few good moves. Frankie and I danced for at least 20 minutes before he went to get us punch. Not once had he looked at other girls. Lara was right, 'he was all mine.'

I made my way to the bathroom, to make sure those crazy curls Rose Marie formed on my head hadn't fallen. Everything was still in place, thanks to almost an entire can of hair spray. My make-up looked great, too. I was starting to appreciate the benefits of a Homecoming Queen sister.

As I looked at my reflection, I couldn't hide a smile at

the pretty girl in the shimmering pink dress. Rose Marie helped me pick it out and I had to admit I looked pretty hot. I would have never been caught dead in a tight dress a year ago, but a lot had changed. The thin straps crossed over the low cut back, and the soft, feminine fabric clung until it ended just at the knee. Mom had doubts about the dress. Dad was furious, but Rose Marie got our parents to back down.

Besides, this gown actually concealed a lot more than what other girls were wearing, especially Summer Powers, whose chest was ready to fall out of her sparkly black tube top. I was shocked, not at what she was wearing, at her date—Jacob Flushman. I was still laughing over that.

I spotted AJ and Krysta when I came out of the bathroom. They looked awkward standing next to the two coolest guys at the dance. They'd told me they had surprise dates; I had kind of suspected they would abduct AJ's brother and his best friend.

The Mikes sneered as they scanned the crowd of freshmen. They probably had lots of better things to do on a Friday night than baby-sit two goofy girls. I looked AJ and Krysta over from a distance. AJ was actually in a dress! I wondered what bribery Krysta used to get her into that thing. Whatever the case, AJ looked pretty as a girl.

Krysta's eyes widened as she spotted me coming toward them. "Love the dress. Jennifer Lopez wore one just like it in *Cosmo*."

"Look at you, girl." AJ grabbed my shoulders and turned me around. "You're a skinny little hottie."

"You clean up nice as a fem, AJ," I laughed.

She batted her eyes and flipped her hair, pretending to be a stupid priss.

"Hey," I asked. "How did you get the Mikes?"

"Mom threatened them." AJ rolled her eyes at their dates. Krysta bounced, nearly jumping out of her heels. "I think, after tonight, we'll be the most popular girls at school."

I giggled. "The Mikes don't look like they're having much fun."

"Too bad." AJ shook her head in mock sympathy.

"They're ours tonight."

"Yeah," Krysta beamed, "and they'll make great pictures. You have to make sure we go in the yearbook with them."

"Ask Lara, she's the one taking pictures tonight." I pointed in Lara's direction after I spotted her out of the corner of my eye.

Lara looked sophisticated. She opted for sleek, low-rise black pants and a modest cut, matching black top. Her long black hair was swept up in a simple, elegant twist. Her black sequined flip-flops made the outfit. And for jewelry, of course, nothing fit better than her camera.

"Yeah, we saw her." AJ tensed. "The Mikes were flirting with her, but she blew them off."

"That's Lara," I said. "She only cares about taking pictures."

Krysta shrugged. "She doesn't act like a slut to me."

I raised my brows, eyeing Krysta and AJ. "She's not a slut. I already told both of you Summer and Jacob started those rumors."

AJ swung her little beaded purse in a menacing gesture. "If I hear anyone talking smack about Lara, I'll shut them up."

"Cool." I looked over their shoulders. "Frankie's coming back. I need to go."

"Good luck." AJ smacked me on the shoulder.

I winced, but not at AJ. Grody Cody bumped into Frankie, almost causing him to spill the punch. Frankie looked ready to pound him.

"Hey, where you been?" His voice was tense. "I almost spilled these, twice."

"Sorry. Girl thing." I batted my eyes and bit my lip. A technique Rose Marie had just taught me.

Frankie broke into a wide grin as he handed me the punch.

"Don't you two make a nice couple."

I turned to see Mrs. Stein beaming. She wore baby's breath in her hair and cradled a flower clutch to her chest. I didn't quite get the Hawaiian strapless sundress she was wearing but since she was my favorite teacher, I decided to overlook her fashion flaws.

She whispered in my ear, "I knew my plan would

work."

My jaw dropped. "You set us up, Mrs. Stein?"

She laughed. "You should be thanking me."

I loved hearing her laugh. She had been doing a lot of that these past few weeks. But best of all, no more depressing thoughts.

"Thanks, Mrs. Stein. But not just for that, for everything." I leaned over and gave her a big hug.

She patted me on the back. "Just doing my job."

"No," I said, "your job is to teach, but you're more than a teacher. By the way..." I tilted my chin. "I finally get equations."

Mrs. Stein squeezed her handbag tighter, the lines of her wide smile were so stretched I thought her face would burst.

"I never had any doubts."

Frankie poked me in the ribs. "Are we gonna dance or what?"

A thrill ran through me at his words. I couldn't believe it. For a moment, I had forgotten the hottest guy in school was at my side.

He tossed our drinks into the garbage and pulled me to the floor for a slow song.

The magical feeling returned as his fingers locked in mine. I wasn't scared or worried, just excited. Tonight I would not embarrass myself. I shared smiles with AJ and Krysta, who had dragged the Mikes onto the dance floor. The blinding light of a camera's flash caught me off guard. I looked up to see Lara.

"If it's ugly," I roared, "I'm deleting it."

She winked from above her viewfinder. "You look beautiful, trust me. No booger picking." She nodded her head toward a cluster of chairs in the back of the gym.

Jacob was sitting with his Gameboy, stretched out with his legs on a nearby chair. Summer looked absolutely bored as she watched her date play his game.

I tapped Frankie's shoulder and pointed in their direction. "Jacob and Summer don't look like they're having much fun."

Frankie shook his head. "That boy needs a reality check."

I shrugged. "I never thought I'd say this, but I kind of

feel sorry for Summer."

"Maybe I should ask her to dance." His lips curved into a mischievous grin.

I pulled back my shoulders and glared. "Maybe you should kiss my butt."

"What?" He leaned in, a grin splitting his lips. "Sophie wants a kiss?"

I pushed on his chest. "Not here." Panicking, I could feel the nervousness shoot through my limbs.

He bent his lips toward mine. "Why not?"

"Mrs. Stein and Mr. Sparks are watching." I tried to scan the room, but his penetrating eyes drew me in. "You do the math."

Trapped by his heated gaze, a thousand different fears seared my mind. I grappled with my brain to find some way out of the inevitable. He was going to kiss me in front of all these people. There was nothing I could do to stop him but, truthfully, I didn't want to stop him.

He leaned in closer, his lips dangerously a breath away. "I'm sick of equations."

Frankie's mouth met mine in one exquisite kiss. His lips were soft, just barely wet from the punch, and oh so nice. Nothing else mattered. Not getting caught by the principal, not the gossip on the dance floor, not even the light from Lara's flash that I knew had captured our kiss. I was Sophie 'So Hot' Sinora, and I was cool.

Next in the Whisper series...

Don't Tell Mother

Don't jump.

My will was not my own. An invisible force pulled me closer toward the edge. Fear kept my limbs at my side, my arteries as lifeless as an empty graveyard. Only my eyes willed themselves to move—down. The earth below was shrouded in white mist, obscuring the distance to the ground, but I sensed the depth. No person could jump and live to tell. So what propelled my foolish feet forward? Was this a dream? Was I already dead? Another step and I knew I would fall.

Suddenly, I felt the ground beneath me give way. The force of the fall sucked my body into a death-grip; the icy wind slapped my face as I raced downward. I could see nothing through the mist, but the bite of the chill wind licked my arms and legs like a thousand burning whips. As the heat increased, the mist dissolved, and to my horror, I saw my final destination—grey, cold and unwelcoming.

I was going to die.

****

"Bob? You're going out with *Bob*?"

My best friend, Sophie Sinora, stared at me in mock horror, the juices of her cafeteria hamburger dripping freely onto her napkin. I'd revealed my shocking secret as she was mid-bite of her processed meat product. Bob Klinek had asked me out, and I'd said "yes".

What made this secret so shocking was that Bob was totally different. He was a skater and a punk. I was the basketball team captain, usually scoring half the team points. Even with that, I considered basketball a warm-up season; I lived for the softball mound. My fast pitch was gaining speed, and my curve ball stumped most batters.

"Forget that he's a freak." My other best friend,

Krysta Richards, twirled a carrot stick between the tips of her polished fingernails, her olive skin glowing unnaturally beneath too much Glitter Glam. "What kind of name is Bob? It's so last century."

I glared at them. "I like his name."

"Didn't you have a cat named Bob?" Sophie's green eyes sparkled with amusement as she tossed her long, chestnut hair behind her shoulder, totally unaware as ketchup carelessly dripped down her chin.

I exhaled. "Yeah, so?"

I knew telling them was a bad idea, but I was trying to stay calm, especially with Sophie. Her eyes had been red and swollen since her BF, Frankie, had moved away last week. Now that she was solo again, I guess I wasn't allowed to go out with anyone, either.

Krysta leaned over and delicately patted Sophie's chin with her neatly folded napkin. With a stroke of her hand, she smoothed her frizzy locks down before slanting a smile in my direction. "Bob is a pet's name."

"Or a freak's name," Sophie said while spewing meat debris onto the lunch table.

Krysta glared at Sophie while making a grand gesture of sweeping the table with her napkin. "Jocks don't date freaks."

"In case you've forgotten," I hissed, "I'm a freak, too. Just like you two."

Which is how we ended up as friends.

We found out about each other's gifts when we were kids. Even though I was only eight, I knew I was different, and I felt their differences, too. Around them, I didn't feel strange, and we pledged to keep our gifts secret.

Sophie scanned the cafeteria, and then leaned closer. She reeked of the nauseating, sweet-smelling school ketchup substitute. "I didn't *choose* to read minds and you didn't *choose* to have visions."

"And I didn't ask for dead people to wake me up all night, but Bob *chose* to dye his hair like a parrot and get a Mohawk," Krysta sneered. "What's with the duct tape on his wrists? Are you going out with a cutter?"

"No, he's not cutting." Bob might have been weird, but my BF didn't slash his wrists. I wouldn't have gone out with him if he did. As far as his hair was concerned, green is our school color. Nothing wrong with school pride.

Krysta laughed. "Then he's too cheap to wear a real bracelet."

She sounded like a rich snob. No one would know by the way she turned up her nose that she lived in a run-down apartment. Her dad was just as poor, if not poorer, than Bob's family. Krysta refused to accept that fact and the few clothes she owned were all designer labels.

I clenched my jaw, trying my best to refrain from saying something I'd regret later, although it was hard not to lay a verbal smackdown on them—very hard.

Maybe if we talked about something else, I'd cool down. "Speaking of our gifts, I had that dream again last night."

Sophie's eyes widened. "The falling dream?"

"Yeah." I shuddered. Maybe bringing up the dream wasn't such a hot idea. I was the type of girl who liked to be in control. Plummeting from the sky toward certain death was not my idea of peaceful slumber.

Krysta bit her bottom lip, hesitating before speaking. "Did you see who it was this time?"

I shook my head in disgust. "I woke up."

Sophie threw down her hamburger. "Why do you keep doing that?"

"Because I was about to crap my pants," I spat. "Do you know how real my dreams feel? If you were racing toward ice, you'd want to wake up, too." I wanted to see who it was more than anyone, but how could I see the person's face, anyway? I was in the body of the falling person. *Wait a minute!* Fear clenched my jaw, and my spine froze. *What if the falling person was me?*

"You never mentioned ice before."

Sophie broke my thoughts. *Thank God.*

"Yeah," I bit back a bitter laugh. "I finally saw the ground this time. It looked shiny and grey, like ice or dirty snow."

Sophie straightened her spine. "I'm staying away from mountains and airplanes until you figure out who it is."

Sophie and Krysta knew my dreams came true. Usually, I have cool dreams. I knew the hottest guy in school would ask Sophie to the Freshman Formal. Last month was the first time I'd ever foretold a death, Krysta's Grammy. I dreamt of her funeral the day before she had a fatal heart attack.

"Now that I am totally spooked..." Krysta tossed me a sideways grin. "Let's change the subject. What were we talking about again?" She tapped her lip a few times, pretending to be serious. "Oh, yeah, tape."

"He likes tape." Keeping my tone even, I tried my best not to let her see I was beyond frustrated. I was ready to drop the subject of Bob. They wanted to judge him before knowing him, so I didn't see any point in getting angry.

Maybe Bob and I didn't look like we fit together. I'd worn my pale blonde hair in the same ponytail ever since I could dribble a ball. I didn't need gobs of makeup or the coolest fashions to look pretty—just jeans and jerseys. Something about the way Bob's green spikes swayed with his stride was kind of mesmerizing. Although I preferred a natural look, Bob's clothes and his hair seemed like an extension of his unique personality. I couldn't imagine him any other way.

"I bet he likes tape," Sophie laughed, "especially when it's ripping the hairs off his arms."

I half-smiled, narrowing my eyes in Sophie's direction, willing her to read the true meaning behind my grin—*Shut your face.* "He doesn't have hair there anymore."

"Nice." Krysta threw back her head. "Can I barf now?"

I sighed, pushing away my half-eaten burger and flexing my knuckles. "I'm leaving before I smack one of you."

"We're just looking out for you, AJ."

Krysta's tone was much too adult, like she was my mother, which made me even less willing to listen.

"Yeah," Sophie said, "like when I liked that loser, Jacob, and you told me to ditch him."

Before she went out with Frankie, Sophie liked this total vomit-heap, Jacob Flushman, but that was way different. Bob had something Jacob didn't—a life.

"Bob's *not* a loser." I closed my eyes and tried to count

to ten, something this stupid therapist Mother took me to told me to do. It wasn't working, because I could hear them snickering about his duct tape. Maybe they'd get tired of me ignoring them and leave.

"He's got earrings all over the place, AJ," Krysta nagged. "I never thought you'd go for a freak."

"Yeah," Sophie blurted, "and speaking of freaks. Your mom would freak if she found out about Bob."

I clenched my forehead. Just the thought of my meddling, manipulative mother getting in the way of Bob and me made the aching vein on my temple throb with a vengeance.

I had another reason to keep Bob away from Mother. Nothing I did was ever good enough. If I brought home an A minus, she wondered why it wasn't an A. If I threw an amazing fast pitch, she complained softball wasn't as fun as watching my brother Mike play football.

He got all the attention and all the cool stuff. The only reason I finally got a computer was because Mike gave me his hand-me-down when Mother bought him a new one. I still wasn't allowed a cell phone. I must have been the only girl in ninth grade without one. Things were about to change; I was tired of playing second string to my brother. This was the year I was going to make my mother treat me with respect.

****

"I heard a boy's voice on the other end of the phone this morning," Mother carefully spread her fat-free margarine across her whole-wheat toast. "Who was he?"

I clutched my Sunday comics to keep from looking up at her. The joints in my fingers felt as if they were encrusted in blocks of ice. I dared not twitch a muscle on my face for fear she'd know what I was thinking.

I'd been so careful. *How did she find out?* I told him not to call me, and I only called him when Mother was in her garden or at the store. This wouldn't have happened if Mother would just let me get a cell phone.

"Bob," I murmured.

"Bob?"

"Yes, Bob." I tried to sound relaxed, unconcerned, but I knew I wasn't convincing. Mother had some kind of a secret, parent radar, that sliced and diced the meaning of every look, expression or thought.

"Well," she purred, "that sounds like a nice, normal name. He must be a pleasant young man."

"Uh." My brow twitched. "Yeah."

"So, is this Bob a boyfriend you haven't told me about?" Her tone transformed from 'I'm a sweet, loving mommy' to 'I want to plague my daughter with guilt for not confiding in me.'

"Well." I shrugged, slowly easing down my paper. "Kind of."

My gaze gradually found hers. If her brows were raised any higher, she could've used them to scrape the ceiling.

"When do I get to meet this Bob?" Her lips twisted into a slight snarl, and then she relaxed her face into a sweeter expression while she smoothed perfectly manicured fingers through her elegant long, blonde hair.

My beautiful mother. The image of perfection.

On the outside.

I wasn't fooled. "Meet him?"

"Why don't you invite him to dinner, Mom?"

My older brother, Mike, was smirking from the other end of the table. During my interrogation, I'd forgotten he was there. By the excited expression on his irritating face, he'd been hanging on every word.

Having Bob over for dinner was the last thing I wanted. Forget that he was a freak. What would he think of *my* family? "I don't think..."

"That sounds like a wonderful idea, Mike." Mother beamed at him, her icy-blue gaze taking on a much warmer hue.

I narrowed my eyes and shot mental daggers at Mike. *Why did I have to have a brother? Why?* Things were supposed to be different now that we were older. Now that he was out of the 'hold my sister down and fart on her face' stage, I thought he was actually maturing.

Guess not.

Mike lowered his eyelids and leered from under his lashes. Oh, yeah, the jerk was having a real fun time putting me on the hot seat. Just last week, he'd been busted stealing a dead cat from the lab room and leaving it on his English teacher's chair.

Even though Mike was in high school, and I was stuck in junior high, gossip traveled fast in our small community. I'd heard all about the cat incident before Mike's principal got a chance to call home, but Mother didn't even put him on house arrest.

Mike was president of the junior class, captain of the tennis team, starting quarterback for varsity, blah, blah, blah. My friends thought Mike was some kind of bronzed, blonde God. Sure, he had muscles; sure he was okay to look at, but underneath...what an irritating, immature creep. According to Mother, Mike could do no wrong.

Meanwhile, none of my accomplishments seemed to matter to her. She hardly ever went to my games. Captain of the girls' basketball team and starting softball pitcher meant nothing to a former head cheerleader. I could score ten points on the court before any of those stupid cheerleaders counted their toes. But as a jock, I wasn't a *normal* girl, or so Mother told me.

"Yeah, I'd like to meet him, too." Mike grinned, smacking a spoonful of cereal like a pig. "I don't remember him from Greenwood. What sports does he play?"

I hoped Mother didn't notice my cheeks were burning. They felt on fire. "Oh, you know, the usual."

"Let's save these questions for Bob," Mother interrupted. "Invite him over this Friday. Is there something wrong, dear?"

She scrutinized my face as I tried not to breathe.

"Don't worry," she smiled. "We'll try not to be too scary."

A word about the author...

A former Texas high school teacher, Tara West is taking a break to raise her baby girl. She enjoyed coaching her writing team and even the hectic deadlines that came with running the school publications. Tara longs for another classroom of her own.

In her spare time, Tara loves to write – anything. She's also obsessed with photography and graphic design. She contributes the cover art for her own novels. She'd love you to visit her at tarawest.com.

Printed in the United States
124749LV00001B/32/P

9 781601 541444